Little Miss Moth

by Amy Le Feuvre

NATAL PUBLISHING LLC
ARS LONGA, VITA BREVIS

CHAPTER I
A NEW HOME

THREE little girls were looking out of the window on a very wet afternoon in March. They were so close together in age and height that sometimes two of them were taken for twins, yet there was a year between each of them. And they were unlike each other in looks.

Charity, the eldest, had a quantity of red auburn hair down her back. She was very lively and talkative, and her eyes were always sparkling with fun and happiness.

Hope, next to her in age, had fair golden hair and blue eyes; she was sweet tempered and rather apt to be an echo of anyone with whom she was.

Faith, the youngest, was a quiet child, with short, dark, curly hair, and thoughtful brown eyes. She had a very sweet little face, but looked fragile and delicate beside her rosy, sturdy sisters.

It was not a very cheerful scene outside the window. One of those quiet, dingy streets towards the outskirts of London, where rows of houses faced each other, all exactly alike, and where the only traffic was the tradesmen's carts rattling along, and an occasional cab or motor. But the little girls were talking fast and happily. The rain beating against the window panes did not depress them. The dark grey sky, the wet pavements, the wind whirling the smoke along the street from the chimneys opposite, the people hurrying by under sodden umbrellas, all interested the six bright eyes.

And at last three voices shouted happily:

"Here she comes, Granny! Here's Aunt Alice!"

They left their post at the window and rushed to the door. Mrs. Blair, their grandmother, who was sitting in an easy chair by the fire, knitting small stockings, sprang up as if she were twenty instead of nearly seventy. She took a small kettle off the hob, and poured the hot water into a teapot.

Tea was laid on a round table in the middle of the room. There was only a loaf of bread and a pot of treacle, but everything was very bright and clean; and the little room looked quite cheerful in contrast to the grey, dingy street outside. There was a canary hanging up in the window, and a handsome black cat sat washing its face on the hearthrug. Bright pictures were on the walls, and in the centre of the table was a big bunch of yellow daffodils.

Now the door opened, and Aunt Alice appeared, with a bright, rosy face; and her three small nieces were instantly hanging round her.

"Oh, Granny, she's got some primroses!"

"She's picked them herself!"

"And there's a parcel—very special for you!"

"Now let me speak, chicks! And first I must shed my wet shoes. Charity, run and get me my slippers from upstairs. Yes, Faith, you can take these out into the kitchen, and ask Mrs. Cox to dry them for me."

Aunt Alice bent down and kissed Granny.

"You do look cosy here. I shall be thankful to have a cup of tea!"

In a few minutes all were gathered round the table, and then Granny opened her parcel, which contained a pound of golden butter.

"There!" said Aunt Alice. "What do you think of that? Old Mrs. Horn sold it to me. They are not rationed in butter down there. And, Mother, dear, I have had a very successful day, and the cottage is sweet. I have seen Sir George, and he will let it for ten pounds a year. Think of it, with no rates or taxes, and a garden big enough to grow our own vegetables, and an orchard with six good apple trees in it!"

"And what about the water?"

"Quite a good well close to the house, and these primroses are out of the orchard, and Mrs. Horn who lives only a field away will supply us with milk."

"What is the cottage like?"

"There is a big kitchen and dairy; the kitchen larger than this; a tiny best parlour, which I don't think we will use at all, and four good bedrooms, and cupboards in every room built into thick walls."

Granny's eyes sparkled as brightly as the children's. "And when can we have it?"

"Sir George said he would have it papered and painted throughout. It is in good repair. His coachman lived there for ten years before he went to the war, and his wife was a 'clean body,' so Mrs. Horn informed me. Poor thing, she died a month after she had left it. She had a weak heart, and she heard of her husband's death suddenly, and it just killed her."

"Did you see Lady Melville?"

"Just for a moment. Sir George sent his love to you. He said it would be like old times to see you again."

There was silence. The little girls were busy eating their bread and treacle, but their ears were taking everything in.

"And is the cottage lonely?" asked Granny.

"No, I don't think so. It lies just off a road. There's not much passing, but, Mother dear, you will revel in the peace and quiet after this!"

Aunt Alice waved her hand out of the window. She was smiling brightly. Granny looked at her rather wistfully. "And you have quite made up your mind to give up your war work and come with us? You don't think I could manage with the children?"

"I am sure you could not, Mother. There will be wood to be sawn, and the garden to be tilled. Sir George has given us leave to gather all the wood we want from his woods, but we can get no man or boy to help us. Mrs. Horn told me that. She is running her small farm without any man at all, her two daughters do everything. The children must make themselves useful."

"And what about their lessons?"

Aunt Alice looked grave.

"I don't know. If we can't find any one to teach them, I suppose I must try myself. There is the village school a mile off."

"No, Alice, I shall not let them sink to that."

Aunt Alice laughed and shrugged her shoulders

"Oh, Mother dear, we won't bring them up with empty brains as well as empty purses! They will have to earn their own living, so they must have a good education."

"Well, we will talk about that later."

"And we'll all have a slice of bread and butter now," said Aunt Alice briskly. Then she turned to the children, and began to tell them of all that she had seen and heard since she had left them two days ago.

And when tea was over, Charity slipped out to the kitchen. She was longing to impress Mrs. Cox with the wonderful new life in front of them.

Mrs. Cox was a thin, gaunt woman who came every day from eight o'clock to six in the afternoon. She cleaned, she cooked, she washed and ironed, and was the children's devoted friend. They were never tired of listening to her stories, but Mrs. Cox always enjoyed very dismal subjects. Funerals and illnesses were her chief topics; and her friends seemed to the children to have had the most marvellous diseases, and the most miraculous cures that they had ever heard.

"Oh, Mrs. Cox," cried Charity, dancing up to her, as she sat at the kitchen table enjoying her cup of tea, "we're going to the country to a house all our own, and no lodgers in the top floors of it, a house with a well, and primroses, and apple trees, and we shall have butter—real butter—every day, and a forest with big trees, and we shall pick up wood in it and light our fires. And Aunt Alice will be home all day!"

Mrs. Cox stared at her.

"Ah, well, yer h'aunt did say to me times was hard, and you couldn't h'afford to go on livin' here, that and the h'air raids—but never did I think you'd all sink down to the country! 'Tis only where folks live in their dotage, or sick children be sent for their 'olidays; nobody with brains or money be content with such a hom'! Why, me sister Ivy went down to a place there, an' were that skeered she's never prop'ly recovered since. She left before the end o' her month; she said when you looked out of the windys, there were nothin' but trees tapping their branches on the windy panes, and earwigs a crawlin' inter the beds, if you please, and you walks miles and never meets a single human soul, an' the nights black pitch, so's the evenings out were a crool joke! Not to speak of mud comin' up your legs over your boots—!"

"Go on—how perfectly lovely!" cried Charity with glowing eyes.

But Mrs. Cox shook her head gloomily, and refused to say another word.

"Granny lived in the country when she was little, and our Dad was born in the country, and when Grand-dad was alive, he kept a school in the country for little boys, and Granny used to love them, and they loved her. And George Melville had curly hair, and Granny used to keep a bag of chocolates in her room for him, and now he's grown-up, and has a big house, and he's going to let Granny and us live in one of his small houses. We're going to be awfully happy in the country, Aunt Alice says everything is nice there."

Mrs. Cox gave an unbelieving sniff.

"Once I went on a Mothers' treat. It rained twelve hours on end—and I sat on a damp log o' wood, and was ill in bed of rheumaticks for a month h'after! Give me a proper Lunnon park for beauty. Why, the park flowers beat the country ones holler!"

Charity left her. Mrs. Cox would not understand the joy of looking forward to a move into an unknown country.

Two hours later, the three little girls were in bed in one room upstairs. Aunt Alice and Granny always slept together.

They were talking hard over the prospect in front of them.

"I s'pose," said Hope with knitted brow, "that we're very, very poor. It's only since Granny and Aunt Alice were doing up sums together in their account books that they said they couldn't stay here any longer."

"No," said Charity; "it was when Faith was so ill the other day. The doctor said Granny must take her to the country, and Granny shook her head. And I heard her say to Aunt Alice after:

"'I should like to have something worth selling, my dear, but I've no more jewels, and all our silver is gone, and the bits of furniture left us are worth nothing.'

"Poor Granny! She wiped her spectacles when she said it, and she always does that when she's unhappy."

"And we do wear out our shoes, and eat a lot," said little Faith with fervour. "If we live in a cottage, p'raps it won't cost so much."

"And perhaps we shall be allowed to run about without shoes and stockings," said Hope; "that would be lovely, like we did at the sea, when Aunt Alice took us to Margate."

"I know one thing," said Charity, rolling round in bed in ecstasy; "I mean to get lost in the wood as soon as ever I can."

"And I shall climb the apple trees," said Hope.

"And I shall sit on the well," said Faith, "and draw water up and down in a bucket all day long!"

"And as for Mrs. Cox," said Charity, "she's only talking of the country she's seen—not of our cottage, which is perfectly beautiful. Aunt Alice says so!"

Then sleep overtook them, and when Granny came up to bed, she paid them her usual nightly visit.

"Poor little souls!" she said. "Life will not be so difficult for us in the country; we may be able to give them more pleasures."

The following days were full of bustle and excitement to the children. They had been going to a small private day school a few streets away, but now they were taken away from it, and Charity expressed a hope that they would never go to another school as long as they lived.

"It's our names," she confided to her aunt; "why did our father and mother give us such names? The girls all laugh at us, 'specially me! 'Charity' means everything nasty. If you live on people's charity, it means you're a nobody, and Charity schools are for the very lowest. I hate my name! I'm glad we're going to the country. Mrs. Cox says we shall have nobody there to notice what we're called."

"I like your names," said Aunt Alice laughing. "Don't be a little goose. Your Mother was a saint, and she got your names from the Bible, and so far from 'Charity' being a name to be despised, it is the greatest of all other names. We are told so, you read the chapter about Charity and see all you ought to do if you're worthy of your name."

"Oh, I know! Granny read it to me once. It is in Corinthians, but I couldn't be like that chapter, no, never!"

She shook her red hair vehemently and danced away. Charity was always jumping or running or dancing; she hated keeping her legs still, and school was a real trial to her.

Granny and Aunt Alice packed day after day. Mrs. Cox asked how they were going to manage in the country if they had no one to clean for them, and Hope asked her aunt anxiously about it, but she was laughed at.

"I am going to stay at home, and do all Mrs. Cox's work. I must, that is why I am leaving my work at the War Depôt. Don't you think I am able to keep a cottage clean, Hope? You will all have to help. Granny is not so young as she used to be, and we must spare her all heavy work."

"I love scrubbing," said Hope happily. "I hope you'll let me do that. Are we as poor as Mrs. Cox is?"

"Poorer, I think," said Aunt Alice cheerfully.

Nothing seemed to depress her, and Granny was just as cheerful, so Hope said to Mrs. Cox, "It will be all right, Mrs. Cox. Aunt Alice says it will. We are going to do everything ourselves. We've got very poor, I don't know how, but Granny always says a beggar is happier than a king! And we shall love it all, I know we shall."

The day came when a cab drew up to the door, and the little girls with their arms full of parcels and baskets followed Granny out of the house in which they had spent most of their lives, and rolled away to the big, bustling station. The journey in the train was a delight to them, and when early in the afternoon they arrived at a quiet little station called Deepcombe, and were told by their aunt that they must get out, they looked round them with shining eyes noting every detail around them.

There was a shabby little cart waiting for them outside the station, and it was a tight fit to pack themselves and their luggage into it. A girl drove it, and she and Aunt Alice walked up all the hills. It seemed as if the road was never going to end, but the children had plenty to see as they went along. Lambs in the meadows; primroses on the banks, and pretty thatched cottages and farmhouses standing back from the road.

Charity was loud in admiration and wonder, Hope asked questions about everything. Little Faith was the silent one, she looked up into the blue sky and across the green fields with a dreamy smile upon her small white face.

Granny bent down to her once: "Are you tired, darling?"

Faith's back ached, but she never acknowledged it. She only smiled up at her grandmother. "It's like heaven, I should think!" was all she said.

Granny put her arm round her. Faith was very delicate, and she was continually in her grandmother's thoughts. Granny often said to Aunt Alice that Faith lived at Heaven's gates, and she was afraid that any day she might slip inside them.

At last they reached the Cottage. It had a white gate which had been freshly painted, and the door stood open; and kind Mrs. Horn had lighted a fire, and put a kettle on to boil and was standing outside the door, ready to welcome them.

The little girls tumbled over each other in their excitement to get inside. It seemed at first like a doll's house to them; the stairs were steep and narrow, and the rooms low, and the windows very small, but they loved the quaint cupboards; and then they ran out into the garden and orchard, and visited the well and picked some primroses, and whilst Granny and Aunt Alice were seeing to the luggage being carried in, their tongues wagged fast.

"It's all beautiful," said Charity, "just like the cottages in story books; and I hope we'll never go back to London again in our lives!"

"And we can pick flowers wherever we see them," said Faith, "without paying for them or having the keepers coming up to see what we're doing."

"Where is the wood?" asked Hope.

Charity began to climb one of the apple trees.

"I think I see some trees over there," she said, pointing to the corner of a field a short distance off. They were going to set off immediately in search of it, when they heard their aunt call them in.

"You mustn't run away," she said; "we're all going to have some tea, and then you must help me get your beds made up. There will be lots to do before we go to bed to-night."

"Is this our furniture?" asked Charity, looking round the room, which had only an empty glass-paned cupboard, a square table, a dresser, and six wooden chairs.

"Yes, we've taken over the furniture left here, but we'll make this kitchen quite pretty with nice curtains, and some cushions and some of Granny's pretty things."

So they gathered round the table for their evening meal, and then till bed-time Aunt Alice kept them all busy.

When they at last went up to the sloping-roofed bedroom where they were to sleep, the little girls were too tired to talk any more.

It was Charity who said just before she dropped asleep:

"To-morrow—we'll find the wood, and then our adventures will begin."

CHAPTER II
FIRST ADVENTURES

THE next day came, and Aunt Alice gave her small nieces permission to go off for the morning anywhere they liked.

"I don't think you can get into any mischief," she said. "Charity has a wise little head of her own, and if you like to go to the wood, and bring back some sticks for the fire, I shall be very glad."

"Aunt Alice seems to guess what we should like to do best," said Hope, skipping over the field as joyfully as the lambs had skipped the evening before.

They crossed the orchard, and found a footpath going through some fields. I do not think any little girls in the whole world could have been so happy as these three were on this bright sunny morning. And then just as they reached the wood, something happened to dim their joy. They heard the pitiful shrieks and cries of an animal in pain.

"Oh, what is it?" asked Faith with big eyes. "Is it a wild beast, do you think? It may be a wolf or a fox!"

"We must go and see," said Charity bravely.

They entered the wood by a narrow footpath, and trod one behind the other. Charity hurried along in front, and very soon found a beautiful brown dog writhing on the ground, with one of its legs fast caught in a gin.

They stood and looked at it with pitying eyes; but not one of them knew how to release it. Faith began to sob as if her heart would break. She never could bear to see the smallest creature in pain, and had often cried over a dead mouse in London.

"Let's call somebody," she cried, "he'll be dead, he's bleeding. Oh call somebody quick!"

"But there's nobody to come in the country, Mrs. Cox says so!" said Charity.

Hope and Faith raised their voices.

"Help! Help! Murder!" they cried, for Mrs. Cox had often told them how cries like that brought the policeman to help.

And then Charity joined them, and suddenly they heard a crackling of branches, and an old man appeared. He had a grey beard and a big shady felt hat over his eyes. A great knotted stick was in his hand, and he had leather gaiters up to his knees.

"Hullo! Hullo! What's doin' here?" he said, in a gruff voice.

Faith seized hold of his hands, and her tears dropped fast.

"It's a poor darling dog got caught in an iron thing. Come and get him out quick! Oh, it's cruel, cruel!"

The old man quickened his pace.

"'Tisn't my Sandy! Eh, sure enough it be, an' I be huntin' for him high and low. Still, my boy! So!"

He put his foot on the gin, and with a wriggle and a cry, the dog was free. He stopped whining and stood before his master trembling from head to foot. The old man knelt down and with his handkerchief began to bind up the poor torn leg. Charity and Hope watched the proceeding with the greatest interest, Faith shut her eyes tight. She was as white as a sheet, and, like Sandy, trembled from head to foot.

But Charity began to talk, she asked the old man his name.

"'Tis just Timothy Bendall, shepherd to Farmer Cratton, an' I be livin' at that small cottage three fields off. An' who be ye little ladies? Strangers in these parts, I reckon."

Charity told him all about themselves, how they had just come from London and had come over to the wood, in the hopes of finding some adventures.

He smiled at her, only half understanding what she said. And then when poor Sandy's leg was bound up, he took him up in his arms, and bade the children "Good morning."

Charity and Hope began to run on through the wood, but Faith stood still, and Timothy looked at her. He was fond of children, and he saw how white and shaken she was.

"You poor little maid, what be the matter then?"

"Oh, will he get well? Is he going to die? Does his leg still hurt him?"

"Bless yer little heart, he will be right as rain in a day or two. Would ye like to come on to my cottage and sit there for a bit?"

"Oh, yes."

Faith stretched out her little hand and took hold of his.

"I don't want to go through the wood, we might get our feet in a horrid trap. Who puts them there? Isn't it very wicked?"

"No, no, 'tis just the boys who will trap rabbits, but they oughter open them by day, an' I'll have a word to say to 'em on that score. Come along, and your sisters will find us when they get through the copse."

"What's a copse?"

"What you call a wood."

"But the boys don't catch dear little rabbits?" Faith's face was so distressed and horror-stricken that the old man tried to soothe her.

Charity, seeing her walk off with the old man, came running back, but Timothy told her he was taking Faith to his cottage to rest.

She looked up into his face very earnestly:

"You aren't a wicked robber or ogre in disguise?" she asked. "For we've read lots of stories about children being carried off in woods."

He shook his head.

"Old Timothy wouldn't harm a hair of your heads," he exclaimed; "and 'tis grateful I be, for you callin' help for my poor Sandy!"

"It's all right," said Charity gravely. "I see you've a good face, and if Faith likes to go with you she can; but we want to pick up firewood for Aunt Alice, and find some more adventures!"

She and Hope spent an exquisite hour in the wood. It was as the old man had said, only a small copse; beyond, were big stretches of coverts, but to the two little girls this wood held all their desires. They caught sight of a couple of rabbits scudding away in the undergrowth to their holes; they picked a bunch of the delicate white wood anemones and primroses; they rooted up some moss, and beautiful bits of young ivy; they collected some fir cones, and then began to gather wood. The fresh smell of the moss and earth around them, and the pure spring air filled their little souls with delight. And then they hushed their breaths to listen to the singing of the birds, and the cooing of a wood pigeon in the distance.

"Oh, Faith is missing a lot!" Hope said. "She was stupid to go off with that old man, instead of coming on with us."

"She looked white and sick," said Charity; "I think that trap frightened her, and the sight of Sandy's bleeding leg!"

They were busy picking up some wood, and tying it into small bundles with string, which their aunt had given them, when they heard a man's heavy step amongst the bushes, then a whistle, and Hope caught hold of Charity with frightened eyes:

"Let us hide, it may be a robber!"

"It's too early in the morning," said Charity sceptically, but she pulled her sister round to the back of a big tree, and both peeped round the corner with anxious, expectant eyes.

A tall, broad-shouldered man came in sight, followed by a big black retriever. He was a gentleman, and Charity took courage, and stepped out of her hiding place.

"Hullo! Whose little girls are you?"

"We've just come here, and we're picking wood for Aunt Alice."

"Then you must be related to Mrs. Blair."

"She's our Granny."

He smiled upon them, and emboldened by his smile, Hope came out and confronted him.

"Is this your wood?"

"Yes. Do you know who I am?"

"The boy who always came for sweets to Granny's room," Charity said.

Sir George laughed delightedly.

"The very same; and I'm on my way to pay my respects to her. Do you think she has any sweets to give me now?"

"No, Granny is too poor, and since the war she says it's wicked to buy sweets; for they take the sugar."

He laughed again.

"You must come up and see my wife. She loves small girls. We've only two boys; and school takes them from us most of the year."

Charity's eyes sparkled.

"We came out to meet adventures," she said confidentially; "and you're the second one we've met. Faith has gone off with the first one."

Sir George was then told about the dog, and the old man.

"Mrs. Cox said we would see nobody at all in the country," said Hope; "but we knew she was wrong, for all the books say you meet people in a wood, and we have."

"So you're fond of books."

"Oh," cried Charity, "we love them! I wish we could buy hundreds of books, and have them in book cases up to the top of the ceiling. When I grow up, I shall keep a book shop, and I shall read them all, every one of them."

"Capital! I'm a book lover myself, and you shall come up one day soon, and spend an afternoon with me and my books."

Charity beamed.

"Thank you very much," she said, trying to speak quietly.

"And what does this little maid like?"

He put his hand on Hope's shoulder as he spoke; and she gave her golden hair a shake, as she looked up into his kind eyes.

"Oh," she said, with determined lips, "I shall be a doctor for animals, 'specially horses. I shall keep one to ride myself, and I shall go riding over the country and make all the sick animals well. I bandaged Dinah's paw the other day when she got her claw hurt, and Aunt Alice said I did it better than she did. And I would have loved to bind up Sandy's leg, but I wasn't asked."

"You're going to be a couple of useful women one day," said Sir George; "and they say in the next generation you're going to rule us all. Whilst your sister is reading my books, you can be visiting my stables. They're rather empty these days, but horses are easier to keep than oil, and I believe we have a rough pony who isn't required now to mow the lawn, and who might be ridden upon by a small girl."

Hope's eyes sparkled.

"Why, you've come along just like a fairy," she said, "only you're a man and not a woman."

"And can't a poor man be a fairy?"

"Yes," said Charity hastily, "of course you can, but I think men are generally magicians."

Sir George gave a nod.

"That's what I am, of course," he said. "Good-bye, I shall see you again soon."

He strode along the footpath, and the little girls watched him out of sight.

Charity drew a deep breath of delight.

"Think what Faith has missed. Oh, Hope, you think he really meant what he said?"

"I'm sure he did. His eyes looked so straight and firm, they didn't wobble at all!"

Then they went on picking up their sticks. And when they had got as much as they could carry, Charity said:

"Shall we go to the cottage to find Faith?"

"It's quite near," said Hope, "but we can't carry all this wood up there. Let her find her way home herself."

They retraced their steps, and when they had got outside the wood, they saw Faith running across the field to them.

She looked quite rosy and happy again. They were so full of their meeting with Sir George and had so much to tell her, that they did not ask her what she had been doing, but at last Faith said:

"Well, you've had a lovely time, but I wouldn't have missed my time for all the world."

"What have you been doing?"

"He took me to his cottage; it's smaller than ours, and he lives there all alone, only once a week his niece comes from the village to cook and clean for him. He has the darlingest kitchen with lovely china plates, and mugs and shells, and a stuffed owl, and pictures of hunting. He was a keeper when he was younger, to Sir George, not like a park-keeper; he used to shoot and take care of dear little pheasants. But now he looks after sheep and cattle. And he gave me a drink of milk, and then he sat and talked to me, and he told me of things I've never heard before!"

"And how is Sandy?" asked Hope.

"He is lying in a basket. Do you think Aunt Alice would let me go and see old Timothy again?"

Faith's eyes were shining. Her sisters laughed at her.

"We're going to Sir George's big house, it will be much more adventure than yours."

But Faith shook her head.

"I've had such a wonderful talk," she said.

Hope looked at her curiously, but said nothing. She and Faith were better friends when Charity was not present. Faith had many quaint fancies which Charity laughed at, but Hope never laughed at Faith when she was alone with her.

When they reached the Cottage, they found that Sir George had come and gone. Aunt Alice and Granny were still very busy unpacking and arranging the house according to their liking. But dinner was ready. Only boiled potatoes, and a piece of cold boiled bacon brought from town, but there was a rice pudding, and the children made a hearty meal, for the country air had made them hungry.

After it was over, Charity went upstairs with Granny to help her sort out some of their clothes and put them into the drawers and cupboards. Aunt Alice washed up the dinner things, and Hope and Faith helped her wipe them dry. Then she said they might go out into the orchard and play there till tea-time.

They went off delighted, and soon found a low apple tree which they climbed, and made themselves a comfortable seat amongst its branches. Then Hope said:

"Tell me more about you and Timothy this morning."

Fan looked very sweet and serious.

"You won't tell Charity, for she may laugh."

"No, I won't tell her. I knew you were keeping something back, from your face."

"Well, I said he lives there alone, but it's not quite true, for he doesn't. Somebody else lives with him. Do you know, Hope, he's been telling me of quite a new God?"

Faith dropped her voice to an awed whisper.

"Oh, Faith, how wicked! 'There is no God but One,'" quoted Hope glibly.

"It isn't, it's all in the Bible. I know God lives in heaven, and Jesus went back to heaven, but this is the God Who has His Home on earth now, and He's called 'The Comforter,' old Timothy said:

"'The Comforter lives with me. He ought to live with you, little lady, for He lives to dry all tears.'

"I was crying, I couldn't help it, at poor Sandy's leg! Did you know there was a God called the Comforter, Hope?"

Hope hesitated: "I believe you mean the Holy Spirit."

"But I thought the Holy Spirit was just a Thing like a clean heart," said Faith; "this Comforter is a real person, just like God and Jesus, and Jesus sent Him to take His place when He went away, because He said the world would be so sad, and Timothy says the sad people miss a lot when they don't know the Comforter, for it's the thing He likes best to do to dry their tears and make them happy. So I promised him when I cried next time, I would ask the Comforter to dry them up. And Timothy says He will come and live with any one of us, and make us good if we ask Him."

"Yes, that's the Holy Spirit," said Hope with assurance; "you ask Granny about it. You are so funny, Faith. I knew you hadn't got hold of a new God."

"His Name is 'The Comforter,'" said Faith decidedly; "Timothy told me so, and he is going to teach me about Him when I go to see him."

Then she lapsed into silence, looking dreamily up into the sky.

Suddenly she said:

"I told Timothy He must be specially for children, for grown-up people hardly ever cry; but Timothy says they're often very sad in their hearts, and nobody knows it but the Comforter."

"Well, we're not going to be sad," said Hope, beginning to swing herself to and fro on the apple branch; "I think it's going to be like fairyland here."

"But we shall have to do lessons," said Faith.

Lessons were a greater trial to Faith than to either of her sisters; and many a tear was shed over the spelling-book and the slate of sums.

"We shan't do lessons for a long time Aunt Alice said to Granny this morning. 'We'll let the children run wild for a bit. It won't hurt them, and then we shall see later about a school for them.' Running wild is so lovely. It means swinging on trees like this, and going into the woods and meeting adventures as we did this morning! Charity and I did best, for we're going to see ponies and books in a big house very soon."

"No," said Faith, shaking her dark curls; "mine is best, for I mean to get to know the Comforter if He will let me, and Timothy is going to show me how to do it."

CHAPTER III
AN INVITATION TO THE HALL

"REALLY Lady Melville is very kind," said Granny, opening a note which had been brought her one morning; "she wants the three children to spend this afternoon at the Hall."

The little girls clapped their hands with delight.

"Sir George didn't forget us. He said he would ask us."

"And shall we stay to tea?"

"And wear our best frocks?"

Aunt Alice laughed at their excitement.

"Yes, wear your best frocks and best manners, and do us credit," she said, but Granny added quietly:

"I used to be told that there were no best manners, for the best ought to be the only ones ever used by us."

It was a bright sunny afternoon, when the little girls set out. It was cold weather still, and they wore their navy serge coats and skirts with white muslin blouses underneath. As Granny watched them go out of the white gate, she said to Aunt Alice:

"I shall break my heart if we have to send them to the village school, they look such gentle little creatures. I always say that breeding tells, and if we are poor, we own some ancestors worth having!"

"Oh, mother dear, I am afraid birth is not of much value nowadays," said Aunt Alice laughing; "they will have to be working women when they grow up; we must not forget that."

Charity and Hope walked along with shining faces. Faith was more sober. She had a kind of feeling that she was not really wanted, only included with the others; and she was a little shy of people whom she had never seen. But the joy of walking through green fields, and of seeing for the first time in her life some tiny calves and foals, and of coming across some cowslips, quite compensated for the little forlorn feeling in her heart. Their Aunt Alice had pointed out the big house on the hill, and told them exactly how to reach it. Three fields had to be crossed, then they kept to a green lane, reached some cross roads, took the turning towards the right and arrived at some big iron gates in a stone wall, and a pretty lodge by the side.

They walked in at the gates, and up an avenue of chestnuts.

"It feels like coming to a fairy palace," said Charity; "it all seems just like a story book, doesn't it?"

The old stone house looked very quiet and still when they reached it. There was a wide flight of stone steps to go up and then a big stone porch to be crossed. Charity was reaching up on tiptoe to ring the great door bell, when the door opened and Sir George came suddenly out.

"Hullo!" he said cheerily. "You're in the nick of time! Which is the one who loves horses? Golden hair, isn't it? Come along with me, I'm just off to the stables, and I'll take you with me. Here, Pitman, take these young ladies to the drawing-room."

Hope followed Sir George delightedly whilst Charity and Faith were taken by an old butler across a big hall into a beautiful room with five or six windows, full of china and all kinds of valuable curiosities. A bright fire was burning, and in a chintz-covered easy chair by the side of it, sat Lady Melville, a book in her hand. She smiled sweetly at the children when she saw them:

"I have heard about you," she said. "Aren't there three of you?"

"Yes," said Charity. "But Hope has gone to see the horses with Sir George. I am Charity and this is Faith. Hope is the middle one of us."

"What pretty names!" said Lady Melville. She shook hands with Charity, but she drew Faith by both hands towards her and kissed her. "It is very kind of you to come and see us," she said; "for this is a dull house when my boys are away. Which is the one who loves books?"

"I do," said Charity, flushing.

Then Lady Melville rang the bell, and when her maid appeared she sent them upstairs with her to take off their hats and coats.

"It is only three o'clock," she said, "so we have a long day in front of us. When you have got rid of your walking things, perhaps Charity would like to go into the library and have a look at some of the books there; and Faith can come and talk to me."

Both little girls liked this arrangement. Faith thought it would be very easy to talk to such a sweet kind lady, and Charity was wild to get at the books.

They were awed by the big staircase and the many rooms they passed; but Lacy, the maid, was very pleasant to them.

"Her ladyship ought to have a little daughter of her own," she said; "it's wonderful how she dotes on girls. Because she has only boys, I suppose. That's the way of the world."

Then she showed them a beautiful oil painting in the corridor, a portrait of two rosy-faced, happy boys, in white cricketing flannels.

"That was painted a year ago. The artist stayed in the house whilst he did it. The tallest is Master Lionel, and the youngest Master Fairfax."

"I wish we had brothers," said Charity, "or that one of us had been a boy. I think I should like to have been the boy."

Then they were taken into a big bedroom, and Lacy smoothed their hair; and when they were ready, took them downstairs again. They passed the library on the way to the drawing-room, and Faith, as she peeped in, and saw the books which lined the walls from the floor to the ceiling, wondered how Charity dared take any one of them from their places. They looked as if they had been built into the walls to stay. But Charity's eyes sparkled.

"Can I look at any book I like?" she said.

Lacy shrugged her shoulders.

"If Sir George has given you leave, you can. This is his room. But I'll show you the books Master Fairfax likes. Master Lionel is no reader. Sir George has a shelf for them over here."

She took Charity to a corner of the room, and Charity sat down upon the floor at once, and began to take the books out of the shelves.

Then Faith was taken on to the drawing-room, where she found Lady Melville working at a lace pillow.

"I have put my book by," she said to Faith, with her sweet smile, "because we are going to talk together. I am not very strong just now, so I cannot walk about much, and when I am tired of reading, I make lace. I have a class in the village for making it, and some of the village girls are learning very quickly."

Faith sat down upon a little chair by Lady Melville's side and watched the bobbins flying to and fro between her white fingers with the greatest interest.

"Now tell me how you like your little cottage, and all about yourselves. Do you like coming to the country?"

"Oh, so very much!"

Faith clasped her small hands tightly in her quaint fashion.

"I didn't know," she said, looking up at Lady Melville with her soft brown eyes, "that it would be quite so beautiful. Mrs. Cox didn't like the country, she said, because there was nobody to talk to, but we have found lots of people already. Do you know a nice old man called Timothy who looks after sheep? He is a friend of mine."

"Yes, he was very ill last winter, and I went to see him more than once. I felt sorry for him living all by himself, and nobody to take care of him."

"But he doesn't live quite alone," said Faith softly. "He has the Comforter living with him. He told me so, and when he sits by the fire in the dark, he feels very close to Him, he told me."

Lady Melville looked at Faith very tenderly.

"Did he tell you that, dear?"

"Yes, he told me all about Him. Because he thought it would be a good thing if He lives with me. I don't know if He will come, but I've begun to ask Him in my prayers. Timothy says that tears bring Him very quickly, but we're so happy that I haven't had much to cry about yet. I expect He is waiting till I really want Him."

"I hope you won't find much to cry about here," said Lady Melville in a bright tone. "Tell me how you amuse yourselves. Are you fond of dolls?"

Faith smiled.

"Yes, I love mine. She's called Violet, but Hope has cut her arms and legs dreadfully, and sewed them up again, playing at operations. Charity doesn't care for dolls; she says they aren't alive, but I feel Violet is, when we're alone together. I dare say she seems stupid to people who don't know her, but she's all my own, and I understand her."

"Yes, that makes all the difference," said Lady Melville. Then Faith found herself telling her all about their life in London, and the school they went to, and how the girls laughed at their names, and how they hoped they would not have to go to the village school here.

"Aunt Alice doesn't like teaching lessons," said Faith, shaking her curly head, "so we don't know what will come to us. We have got to learn to be clever, Aunt Alice says, because when we grow up we must work for our living; but being clever is very difficult, and I don't think I shall ever learn it."

"What do you want to do when you grow up?" asked Lady Melville.

Faith's face grew downcast.

"I'm 'fraid I don' know. Aunt Alice says 'time enough yet' and 'something will come.' Charity and Hope have quite settled themselves. I think I'd rather be a mother with about ten little children, all girls, and mostly babies, that I could nurse. But Hope says that is silly, for you can't earn money when you're nursing babies!"

"Oh, yes, you can," said Lady Melville, touched by this old-fashioned, anxious-faced child; "you can be nurse in a hospital for sick babies, or you can be a governess and look after little children, or a nurse in a private house, or you can help in a holiday home or a convalescent home. If you love little children, you will find lots of places open to you when you grow up."

"Without my being very clever?" questioned Faith.

"Yes," said Lady Melville, "and perhaps you won't have to earn any money at all. Perhaps you will have a husband who will do it for you."

"I am rather frightened of men," confessed Faith, "except Timothy. I'm not a bit frightened of him."

Lady Melville laughed.

"Now we won't think any more of your grown-up life, but of how you are going to enjoy yourself in the country. And I am going to think of this problem of lessons. I know a very nice girl about five miles from here. She used to be a teacher in a big London High School, but she wasn't very strong, and had to come to the country to live. She takes care of her invalid mother, but I believe she would be able to cycle over to you, and give you some lessons every morning. Would you like that? I think I must talk to your Granny about it."

Faith was not sure whether she would like it. And in a moment she looked up into Lady Melville's face rather coaxingly.

"You won't hurry about it too fast, will you, please? For Aunt Alice says we can have holidays till she thinks of something, and it is so lovely not having lessons. The children in Heaven don't have lessons, do they? I do so often wish I was playing with them."

"I don't know, I am sure," said Lady Melville, trying to look very grave; "sometimes I think all the lessons we have failed to learn on earth will be finished in Heaven."

"Oh, dear me!" sighed Faith; and then Lady Melville laughed so brightly that Faith laughed too.

And at that minute Sir George put his head in at the door.

"We've done the stables," he said, "but after lunch there is going to be a riding lesson up and down the drive, and the pony wants to see which young lady sticks on his back in best style. Where is Carrots?"

Faith laughed gleefully.

"That's what she's always called at school. She's reading all your books in the book-room."

"I must have a look at her."

Sir George disappeared.

"Do you think you could find a name for me?" questioned Faith wistfully. "We do hate our names so?"

"Oh, I think it's the sweetest little name!" said Lady Melville. "I should be very proud of it if I had it. I think I should try to live up to it."

"How?" asked Faith.

"Well, what does it mean?"

"Tell me."

"Faith is the belief or trust we have in anyone. Who do you trust most?"

Faith thought hard.

"Granny, and Aunt Alice."

"Nobody else?"

Faith nodded.

"Yes, God."

"Then, darling, if you have faith in God, you have everything that you need in this world and in the next. Never doubt God, He will never fail, it is only our faith that fails. And you are called Faith, so you can always remind yourself by your name of the faith you must have in God."

"And the Comforter," said Faith very softly to herself. She did not quite understand Lady Melville's words, but she understood when she grew bigger.

There was no more quiet talk, for tea was brought in, and Sir George came back, leading by the hand both Charity and Hope, who looked perfectly radiant.

And then they had a very merry tea. Sir George delighted Faith by calling her "Curly."

From that time the little girls were always called "Carrots," "Goldenhair," and "Curly," and they tried very hard to make everyone else use those names. After tea, the pony came round, and each one of them in turn had a ride on him. Hope proved to be the most fearless rider. Faith tried to enjoy it, but she had to fight with her fears, and she was relieved when her turn was over.

When half-past six came, three very happy children walked back over the fields home. Their tongues went fast.

Charity had found an old book of Grecian fables and stories which perfectly entranced her. She told the others of some of them as she walked along.

"And Sir George says I can come to his library any day I like and read there."

"And I can ride the pony every day if I like," said Hope. "Oh, isn't it a glorious place with so many dogs and horses?"

"I like the horse," said Charity. "I mean to get rich when I grow up. I shall make myself rich like other people do. I shall save every penny I earn and put it into the bank and buy a house like Sir George's, and have a big library and books just like his."

"But you always said you would keep a book shop."

"I shan't now. I shall have a library."

"I liked the house," said little Faith, "at least it was too big and grand for me, but I didn't mind it as much as I thought I would, for Lady Melville was so nice. I loved her best. I should like to live with her always, with her and with old Timothy!"

"That's just like you," said Charity a little contemptuously, "you're always for people instead of things!"

"Well, I don't care. I do love them better. I like Lady Melville better than a book!"

Faith could speak scornfully sometimes. Hope put in her word. Charity and Faith often quarrelled, and she made peace between them.

"And I think animals are the nicest things in the world," she said. "I shall have lots of ponies and dogs when I grow up."

Then the cottage was reached, and Granny and Aunt Alice were told of the delightful time they had had.

"I knew they would enjoy themselves," said Granny; "Sir George always had a weak spot in his heart for children even as a boy; and his wife seems just as kind."

"Lady Melville said she was coming to see you in a day or two," said Faith; "she knows somebody who may be able to teach us lessons!"

"Ah, that will be first-rate," said Aunt Alice; "if she can help me with that difficulty, I shall be deeply grateful."

The little girls looked at each other. They did not think that they agreed with their Aunt.

They helped Granny by running errands to the village, and each one had her own duties about the house. Charity helped her Aunt to wash up after each meal; Hope dusted all the rooms; and Faith cleaned the brass door handles, and taps, and kept them bright. But they had a great deal of time for play, and whenever it was fine, Aunt Alice encouraged them to be out of doors.

One afternoon Faith was coming back from the village. She had been to the post office to get some stamps, and she was just turning the corner of the road when she saw on a wide piece of grass that edged it a gipsy van. An old horse and a donkey were grazing by the side of it. Now, if there was anything that the little girls really loved, it was a caravan of any sort. They all thought that if they lived in one they would be as happy as the day was long. And Faith's eyes brightened as she came near. Then she saw a little bare-footed boy standing in the road, and crying as if his heart would break.

Faith could not pass him without asking him what was the matter. And then he pointed to a broken jug of milk in the road.

"It was Mother's milk," he sobbed, "and Dad is away, and she's ill, and I've no money for more."

"Don't cry, dear," said Faith. "I've got two pennies in my pocket. Could you get some more milk with them?"

He looked at her with his sharp little eyes, but seized the pennies she held out to him, and taking hold of a tin can on the grass, he tore back along the road as fast as he could go.

Faith stood still admiring the van, which was painted green, and had white muslin curtains at the small windows tied with blue ribbon. Then she heard a weak voice calling:

"Dan! Dan!"

And acting on the impulse of the moment Faith climbed up the steps of the van and looked inside:

"Your little boy will soon be here; he had an accident with the milk, and he's gone to fetch some more."

A woman raised her head from a narrow bed which seemed to take up nearly all the space inside. A little boy of about two sat on the floor munching an orange.

The woman had dark hair and flushed cheeks.

"I'm so thirsty," she moaned, "and oh, so miserable! Who are you?"

CHAPTER IV
CHARLIE'S RAFT

FAITH lost all feeling of shyness in her desire to help this sick woman. She came up to the bedside, and looked at her with her eyes full of pity.

"I'm Faith Blair. We've only just come to live in a cottage here. Can I get you a drink of water?"

The woman pointed to a jug on a shell.

"There's a drop o' cold tea there. I'm never to get up no more, the doctor's told me. He's going to try to get me in the 'Firmary, an' I will not go. My Jim has had to join up, but I promised him I'd keep the van till he comes back, and I want Dan back. He must put the horse in and we must be off!"

She spoke breathlessly. Her cheeks were sunken and she was so thin that all her bones showed through her skin.

Faith got the jug of tea, and poured it out into a cup. She gave it to the woman, who drank it eagerly, then sank back on her pillow as if she were quite exhausted. Then as Faith watched her, the tears came to her eyes, and rolled down her cheeks. She wiped them away with the corner of the sheet.

"Nobody to care for me!" she muttered. "My Jim is away, and when he comes home, I'll be lyin' under the earth like a dog!"

"Oh, but you'll be in heaven," said Faith eagerly; "that will be only your body, and may I just tell you what old Timothy has told me? You needn't be alone or unhappy, for the Comforter will come and stay with you. He is God, you know, and He loves unhappy people. He dries their tears and comforts them. Would you like Him to come to you now? He lives in our world, nowhere else and nobody wipes tears away like Him, Timothy said so."

The woman looked at Faith's eager little face. "I used to hear about them things. I weren't born in a van. I lived proper with my father and mother in a small farm, and Jim used to mend our pots and pans. Oh, he were a handsome boy! An' we was wild to marry, so we just stole off, and I've never been home since. I used to go to Sunday school and church!"

"And have you got a father and mother?" asked Faith.

"No, they've both died."

"Then you're like us; our father and mother died, but we live with Granny. Oh, don't cry! You're beginning again. Do have the Comforter. Timothy says you ask Him to come, and He comes——do ask Him!"

The woman shook her head.

"I haven't said my prayers for years, but I'm scared to die, an' the doctor says both my lungs is gone; you say a little prayer, dearie. It won't do no harm, and p'raps God will be merciful."

So Faith knelt down. She was so much in earnest that all shyness had left her.

"Please, Lord Jesus, will you tell the Comforter to come here quick, for He's wanted. Timothy says You promised to send Him to everybody when You went away. And please let Him comfort this poor sick woman, for Jesus' sake. Amen."

It was only a child's prayer, but it reached Heaven as all such prayers do, and a look of relief and peace crept over the woman's face.

"A prayer said over one always does good," she murmured; and then they heard little Dan clambering up into the van with milk.

She drank it eagerly, and told the boy to put the horse in the van, and drive on as fast as he could.

"I won't be taken into the 'Firmary," she muttered.

So Faith wished her good-bye, and slipped down, and went home.

Charity and Hope were in the garden. She told her story to them. Charity was very interested.

"What was the van like inside? Oh, I wish I had been there! How did you dare to do it? They might have driven off with you, and we should never have heard of you again."

"I should like to have gone," said Faith. "The poor woman had no little girl to do anything for her. The inside wasn't nearly as nice as the outside, it was stuffy and untidy, and not very clean. There seemed no room for anything."

"Here's Granny. Let's tell her about it."

Granny was coming to the cottage door to get a breath of fresh air, but when she heard Faith's story, she did not look very pleased.

"You ought not to have gone in, Faith. She might have been ill of an infectious fever. I don't like it at all. You must never do such a thing again! You are getting too independent."

Faith hung her head.

"What did she say to you?"

Faith told as much as she remembered; but she was shy of telling anybody about her little prayer or of what she herself had said to the woman, and Granny said:

"It was your spirit of curiosity which led you there; and if the woman hadn't been very ill, she might have been very angry at your going in, when you had not been asked to do so. You must never do such a thing again—promise me. Has the van gone away?"

Faith nodded.

"I saw Dan get the horse and fasten it in. They had a grey donkey, too. It followed the van all by itself. They were just moving away before I came into our lane. I'm sorry, Granny, I won't go in again, but I expect I shall never see another van."

"You may see several," said Granny. "I hear there is a common near here where they always encamp, and I won't have any of you go near them."

"Do gipsies steal children now?" asked Hope.

"They wouldn't steal any of you," said Granny with a little laugh; "you are not worth the risk!"

She went indoors again, and Charity said a little indignantly:

"Granny thinks nothing at all of us, but they might steal us, and make us their servants."

"Wouldn't it be fun?" said Hope with gleaming eyes. "And we would eat rabbits in a pot over a bonfire, and live in the fields always. Oh, I wish our home was a van!"

"I like this cottage better," said Faith gravely; "that woman looked most uncomfortable, and her bed was all in a muddle!"

Faith heard no more of Dan and his mother, but she did not forget them, and every night prayed for the sick woman.

Lady Melville was as good as her word. She came to see Granny, and Aunt Alice went over to the neighbouring town to see this governess who might help them.

Every day got warmer and longer. The children soon became friends with the neighbours round. The rector had no family. He was an old man, and his wife was very rheumatic, so was confined to the house a great deal, but the doctor, who lived at the other end of the village, had a little boy who was very delicate, and one day Hope and Faith met him in the village shop buying sweets.

Hope made friends with him by telling him which sweets she thought were the nicest. He was a slim little boy, with brown hair and pale face, and when he come out of the shop, he said:

"My name is Charlie Evans. What's yours? I saw you all in church last Sunday. I don't always come to church. I have headaches."

He said it with an air of pride. Faith looked at him pityingly.

"And don't you go to school?"

"No. I do lessons with mother, and she hates them, and so do I."

"And so do I!" said Faith eagerly. "But we shall have to begin them soon."

"Come and see my rabbits," Charlie said.

The little girls hesitated.

"We won't come to-day, till we ask Granny," said Hope; "but we'll come to-morrow, if she'll let us. Faith went to see some gipsies the other day and she didn't like it."

Charlie turned to Faith.

"Did you? What were they like? Dad told mother he was going to get a sick gipsy out of her van into hospital. She had nobody to look after her, but she went off before he could move her. Gipsies hate being taken care of!"

"Yes," said Faith; "that was the woman I saw. I'm so sorry she went away so quick! She seemed so ill, and so alone."

"I wish you were boys," said Charlie, looking at them with dissatisfaction. "I do want boys to play with so much. Do you know Lionel and Fairfax at the Hall?"

"No," said Hope. "I expect we shall know them, when they come home for the holidays."

"They won't think anything of you," said Charlie rather rudely; "they won't even let me play cricket with them, because I can't run fast enough."

"P'raps we can run faster than you?" Hope said.

Charlie looked gloomily at her, then he brightened up.

"I've got a lovely raft I made all myself on a stream under the willows," he said; "sometimes I go out on it all day to escape Indians."

Hope and Faith pressed nearer him.

"If Granny says we may play with you, will you let us play that?"

"It isn't play," said Charlie with sparkling eyes; "it's a real hard work. I take cargo with me—live cargo!"

Then he walked off and waved his cap in the air.

"If you want to join Captain Charles on his voyage to the Treasure Islands, you'll have to sign on before next Wednesday. The voyage begins on Thursday. That's the first day of my Easter holidays, and Mother and I mean to have three weeks' holidays if Father agrees, and the voyage will last three weeks."

Hope and Faith ran home in the greatest excitement. When Charity heard of the raft, she was determined to know Charlie as soon as possible. And when Aunt Alice heard of it, she said to Granny:

"Mrs. Evans told us of her delicate boy when she called the other day; there is no harm in the children playing together."

So when a little note came from Mrs. Evans, asking the three little girls to lunch on the next Wednesday, they were allowed to go, and went off to the doctor's house in high spirits.

Charlie welcomed them warmly. He took them to his schoolroom and showed them some silkworms and guinea pigs.

"Are these your live cargo?" asked Hope.

He looked at her sharply.

"I have a good deal more than these. Are you going to sign on?"

"I am," cried Hope delightedly.

Faith echoed her words, but Charity demurred.

"Look here," she said; "I always like fair play. One man doesn't want three servants."

"Crew," said Charlie; "you'll be the crew."

"Yes, I know," said Charity, her nose rather high in the air, "and if the Captain chooses, he can flog his crew and put them in irons. I've read all about it, and if they mutiny, what then?"

"They'll have to walk the plank," said Charlie, loftily.

"Oh, what fun!" exclaimed Hope.

"Well, you can do it," said Charity, "but I'm not going to do it; so I shall just be the Captain's wife."

Her audacity struck the three other children dumb.

"Then the wife stops at home," said Charlie, when he had recovered himself.

He had a weak body but a strong spirit.

"A Captain never takes his wife to sea, never!" he said.

"Oh, yes," said Charity, "when he finds her on a desert island and marries her, he brings her to his ship and they sail on together. You found me on the island. Don't you remember? You went to sleep, and when you woke up and you saw a strange shoe, it was too small for any man so you knew it was a woman's, and then you took it in your hand and went along to look, and suddenly you came upon me sitting in a bower with a crown of flowers in my hair, and I told you I had been shipwrecked, and I was Queen of the Island, and if you dared hurt me, I had an army of monkeys who would come down from the trees and kill you. And then we settled together to get married, and you took me away in your ship the next day."

Hope and Faith hung on Charity's words with open mouths and eyes. Charlie set his lips firmly together.

"I don't remember anything about it," he said. "I shall want three to make the crew. One is the cook, the other the one who rows, and the other who cleans and does the dirty work."

Charity set her lips tightly too.

"I'm not going to do what I am told by a boy no taller than myself," she said. "I'm your wife, and I'll promise to be the cook too. But I must be the wife first, and you and I must consult together about everything! And if you won't make me your wife, I'll turn into an alligator and upset the raft, and pull you all into the water. I really will, I know how to do it."

Charlie looked at her with an uncertain eye. But they were called to dinner, before anything could be settled, and as Charlie sat opposite to Charity, he was weighing in his mind the desirability of making her his wife. Hope and Faith looked easy to manage, but he did not want mutiny on his raft, nor did he want it upset, for he thought of his live cargo.

After dinner, they went back to the schoolroom, for the signing on must be accomplished.

"I'll join you as your wife, and it will be ripping," said Charity. "I've lived on a desert island, so I know how to turn my hand to anything; but I won't be one of your crew. I should mutiny the first five minutes, and remember we would be three against one. And I'm sure I could tie your legs together, and arms too, if I were to try; and you would be just a bundle to be sat on, while we went on and had the most thrilling adventures!"

Charlie felt the modern woman too much for him.

"All right," he said; "but if you're my wife, and contradict my orders, I'll land you on the first island we come to, and leave you there. Now, you two crew, sign on. Your names will be Bolt and Ben."

Hope and Faith signed their names on a crumpled bit of paper which set forth that for the whole of the voyage they obeyed the Captain in every particular, and stuck to the raft through every danger. Charity looked on with smiling superiority. But Charlie produced another piece of paper for her.

"A wife has nothing to sign," she said.

"Oh, yes," said Charlie, in a masterful tone: "A wife always signs in a church book after she is married, to make sure she means what she says when she promises to obey her husband and to serve him."

Charity pouted.

"I did that when we were married on the island."

"No, you didn't, for there was no proper church or prayer-book or clergyman," said Charlie quickly, "and you'll have to do it now, and then we shall be quite ready for to-morrow. And my ship sails punctual at eleven o'clock—all aboard by half-past ten."

"Oh, sign, Charity! It will be fun!" cried Hope.

And very reluctantly Charity read and signed the following declaration:

"I promise to obey and serve my husband for the whole of the voyage and until death us do part."

But before her signature, she added the words:

"If I think well."

And as Charlie did not see what she had written till after it was done, he was after all worsted by the woman.

Then they all went out into the garden, and down to the stream where the raft was moored.

It was quite big enough to hold them all, and the stream was just wide enough to let it go floating along without touching the banks. Charlie told them that the stream turned into a river, a mile or two along the fields.

"And then the river goes into the sea; so there's nothing between us and the real ocean, and we can go on for ever."

"Till we reach the Treasure," said Hope, "I hope we shall reach something, Charlie!"

Charlie nodded mysteriously.

The little girls went home in high spirits.

Granny looked slightly alarmed when she heard of what they intended to do, but Charity relieved her mind.

"The stream is so narrow, Granny, that we could step off the raft on the bank, any minute we wanted to, and oh, it will be such fun!"

Granny remembered the pranks of the boys in olden times, when she had so many of them in her house, and smiled.

"It is good to be young," she said.

"And the poor boy is prevented from a great deal of pleasure," said Aunt Alice; "Mrs. Horn was telling me about him. He will never make a strong man, they say."

"He has got a very strong spirit," said Hope; "or is it his soul that is strong and makes him like ordering girls about?"

"What's the difference between a spirit and a soul?" asked Faith.

"Oh, children, let us get away from such discussions," said Aunt Alice laughing; "they are too difficult for us altogether."

The little girls said no more, but they anxiously looked forward to the next day. Suppose it should rain?

Faith was snubbed when she suggested such a thing.

And when the day dawned it was a sunny Spring day.

There were no happier little girls in the world than Charity, Hope and Faith, as they started for the Doctor's house. Aunt Alice gave them a package of egg sandwiches, and some thick slices of bread and jam.

"Go and enjoy yourselves," she said, "but I expect you all back by six o'clock in the evening."

"And by that time," said Faith thoughtfully; "we shall have been a long sea voyage and back, and perhaps we shall come home laden with treasures!"

"Anything may happen," said Charity with fervour, "the very best, or the very worst!"

And so they marched away to meet their adventures.

CHAPTER V
THE PIRATE

PUNCTUALLY at eleven, Captain Charlie's raft with its live cargo, crew and Captain and wife, started for its voyage down the Adderbrook. Every few yards added fresh excitement to the crew. There were frogs, and tadpoles to be seen scurrying out of their way, ducks taking an airing filled the air with their quacks, as they hurriedly made for land; once a water rat sprang on board, but hurriedly splashed back into the stream, when he was greeted with frightened screams.

"Just like girls!" said the Captain scornfully.

"Don't you know a crocodile when you see it?" retorted his wife. "I suppose you will call it a rat! As if we have rats in mid-ocean!"

Several times the raft threatened to upset. The little girls had to be most wary in their movements. Of course such moments were the result of violent storms, when waves sought to engulf them, and the Captain's wife seemed to aid and abet the rough elements when she could. More than once she had to be called to order by the Captain.

They passed through two open fields, and then came to where the willows and rushes bent over the stream and made it very difficult navigation.

The crew had to lie flat on their chests to prevent the willow branches hitting them in the face. But every difficulty was an added delight, and when the Captain struck a gong, and said it was time to dine, and they must land on a desert island and do it, they scrambled ashore with joy.

The raft was tied securely to a tree trunk, and under a white hawthorn tree, the voyagers spread out their lunch and made a hearty meal.

Charlie's mother had given him bacon pasties and cake, and biscuits and cheese—enough for them all. He was not a greedy boy, and was quite willing to share. Charity undertook to divide everything with equal fairness, and in this way every one was more than satisfied.

Up to now they had seen very few people. A boy driving cattle in the distance was an Indian chasing buffaloes; an old man with a dog was a chief with his wolf hound.

But when they took to their raft again, their sharp eyes spied a fisherman some distance away with his line across the stream.

"Now you'll hear him swear," said Charlie, with a delighted chuckle. "I know what fishermen are like. I've passed them before."

"He isn't a fisherman," said Hope; "he's a pirate looking out for ships from his island."

"It's a pity we have no gun to blow him to pieces! My dear husband, put a bit more strength into that old punt stick of yours! Let's rush down the stream and pull hold of his line—perchance we may pull in the pirate to his death!"

So all four got hold of their oars, and by dint of prodding the banks in punt-like fashion, the raft began to quicken its pace. The fisherman saw them before they reached him and pulled in his line. He did not swear but laughed heartily as the raft approached.

"Who the dickens is this?" he asked. "Here, hi, don't pass me by! Is there room for me on board?"

He was a tall, broad-shouldered young man.

Charlie threw a ferocious look at him.

"You're a pirate, let us pass!"

The young man had stopped the raft with his foot. Charlie was rather exhausted with his efforts, and the little girls were panting for breath.

"If I'm a pirate, I beg to tell you that this water is mine, and that you are my prisoners. You'll land at once, and forfeit your ship."

With a quick, dexterous stroke, he had seized hold of the rope, and drawn the raft close to the bank.

Winding it round a tree stump, the discomfited voyagers found their passage stopped.

Charity looked up into the pirate's face. She saw that his eyes were twinkling, and she felt reassured.

"The ocean is free to all," she said boldly.

The young man pointed to a board close by.

"Private water. Trespassers will be prosecuted."

And then Charlie saw that he had brought his raft along the wrong bend of the stream. He had seldom before come as far as this.

For a moment the little Captain looked perplexed.

"We are on a peace voyage," he said, "otherwise with cutlasses and guns we would make short work of you. We are searching for an island called 'Tarjak,' and for treasure thereon."

"Ah," said the young man in a mysterious tone, "now you've come to the right party. I know the very spot and will lead you to it, if I may share in the booty."

"He means treachery!" said Charity in a loud whisper.

"I've got you in my power!" said the young man sternly.

Charlie and the little girls hastily consulted together.

"We'll just let him join us," was Charlie's decision.

Then he turned to the stranger.

"Now will you lead us?"

"I'll tow you along," was the cheerful reply. "You have spoilt my fishing, but I'll take you straight to a treasure island such as you have never seen before."

In a very short time, this amazing young man was marching along the banks rope in hand, and the raft was being towed along without any effort on the part of the crew. They gave themselves up to the delight of it, for all small backs and wrists were aching, and it was delicious to be towed along so swiftly, without any effort.

And presently the stream widened considerably and a veritable small island appeared. The Pirate used the oars now, and stood in the middle of the raft himself. He brought it to the edge of the island and told the children to get out.

To their delight there was a tiny thatched hut in the middle of it.

"Years ago," said the pirate, "I landed here in a small boat, having been shipwrecked, and having lost all I possessed. I built myself this hut and lived here in peace, quitting it for rougher waters and sea fishing occasionally. For the most part I lived on fish. One day I was digging for bait, when I stumbled on a—a cache, and in a certain spot on this island is one hidden now. Treasure is in it. If you have brought spades, dig away till you find it. I will give you a clue. Four paces from Security, an arm's length to the right, dig for two feet down!"

"We haven't any spades," said the little girls. "The Captain has the only one."

The young man went into the hut, and soon appeared with a pitchfork and two spades of very small proportions.

"And now," said Charity, "where is Security? It must be the hut, of course!"

In a very few minutes each child was digging four paces from the hut. But Charlie began to flag, whereupon the young man whispered something to him.

"Your Captain is ill," he said; "he's going to rest. I'll take his place."

Charlie sat down on the step leading to the hut and watched the others with a rather bitter face. It was hard to be bowled over so soon, just when he would like to prove his strength to be superior to the girls.

Digging went on steadily, but the three little girls made slow progress.

The young man dug too, but he presently said, "I'll give another clue:"

"By the side of a singer's home, a hand's span from the base."

The little girls were completely puzzled. Charlie's bright eyes roved to and fro. At last his face lightened.

"I have it. A singer's home is a bird's tree, and the base is the trunk of it. There's only one tree which it can mean, and it's the ash tree between Bolt and Ben."

Charity made a rush to the spot, and Charlie sprang up declaring he was quite rested. He and the three girls all attacked the ground round the ash tree, and the young man quietly slipped into the hut, leaving them at work.

It was not long before Charity's spade hit against something hard. Then four eager pairs of hands dragged it to light. It was a rusty tin box tied with string and sealed.

Charlie took command as Captain, and cut the string with his clasp knife. His face was solemn as he did it, but the little girls' faces bubbled all over with curiosity and delight.

It was hard to open, but at last the lid gave way, and then Charlie very carefully lifted out the contents.

Four black farthings, a blue marble, and two peach stones.

Faith's face fell; she was dreadfully disappointed. She had really expected to find it full of precious stones.

Charity danced up and down.

"Golden sovereigns, a blue jewel worth a million pounds, and seeds of a pomegranate that grew in Paradise!" she cried.

Charlie turned to her with an approving face.

"You are right, my wife, wonderful treasure indeed! Does the Pirate mean to let us carry it off?"

"The Pirate invites you to a meal. He is tired of a very lonely life and welcomes treasure seekers to his home."

It was the young man who spoke. The children dashed into the hut, Charlie clutching his tin box. There another surprise awaited them.

A kettle was boiling merrily. A cake was on the table, and some ham sandwiches. The Pirate had cups and saucers, and was measuring tea into a brown teapot.

"We have no cow on the island, but we have sugar and good tea. Let us fall to!"

It seemed like magic. The children sat up round a little table and they had a merry meal. After it was over, the treasure box was produced and the treasures divided. The Pirate took one of the peach stones. Charity took the other.

"I as Captain's wife have first choice," she said. "I am going to plant this wonderful seed, and perhaps it will spring up into a magic tree which will reach the sun."

Charlie gave Hope and Faith a farthing each.

"A guinea for Bolt and Ben," he said. "I being Captain keep the blue diamond and a guinea, my wife can have the other."

Then the Pirate pulled out his pipe, and sitting cross legged on the ground told them the most wonderful story of how the treasures had been obtained and hidden away. The children listened breathlessly, but at last the Captain said it was getting late, and they must go. The Pirate took them back to their raft, and then he surprised them again. He got out a very small boat from under the willows, tucked himself into it, and fastening the rope of the raft to his painter, rowed gaily off down the stream, towing the children back to the spot where he found them. Then he bade them good-bye.

"We shall never meet again most likely," he said, "but I warn you to keep to your own waters. There are other pirates who would make short work of you should they find you where I did!"

The children waved their hands gaily to him. Charlie was supremely happy, and content at the result of his voyage after treasure, and all their tongues wagged fast as they made their way down the stream towards Charlie's home. It was nearly six o'clock when they got there, so the little girls bade their new friend a hasty good-bye.

"It has been perfect—simply perfect!" said Charity, and the others echoed her words.

They ran home then as fast as they could, and told Granny all of their adventures.

"Who do you think the Pirate can be?" Faith asked. "He has such nice kind eyes, but a very grave face."

Granny said she could not possibly tell, and Aunt Alice could not help them.

But the next day the rector's wife paid a long call. Charity happened to be in the room, and though she was as quiet as a little mouse she kept her ears wide open, and when she was alone with Hope and Faith she was quite excited.

"I believe Mrs. Webster was talking about the Pirate, I believe she was! She told Aunt Alice she had a little grandson staying with her last week, and she wished she had asked us over to tea with him, as he was so lonely. And then she said that Fred Cardwell had been so good to him. He had taken him off fishing with him several days, and had entertained him on an island which the little boy had loved. She asked Aunt Alice if she knew the Cardwells, and I pricked up my ears and listened hard. Aunt Alice said no, and she said Fred Cardwell lived with a very cross, ill father—I think he's a squire, like Sir George, and they live about five miles from here. The father is parry—something—a long word, and Fred had to come home and look after him, and he's no mother or brothers and sisters, and Mrs. Webster said it was a terrible life for him, and it made him gloomy, and he doesn't go anywhere or won't know anybody, but he likes children and she said her little grandson loved him. Don't you think Fred may be our pirate? Because there can't be lots of islands about, and perhaps that was why he had cake and tea in the hut, he had put them there when the little boy was with him!"

Charity paused for breath.

"I wish we could see him again," said Faith.

"We'll keep a sharp look-out along the roads when we walk," said Hope. "Mrs. Cox wasn't at all right about the country. We do meet people very often, and we may meet him."

"We'll ask Lady Melville if she knows him when we see her next," Charity said; "and now I'm going to plant my magic seed. Come and see me do it."

So Hope and Faith accompanied her to the little garden, and she planted it just below their bedroom window.

"Perhaps it will be like Jack's beanstalk, and grow so high that we can step out of our window on to its branches," said Hope.

"It's sure to be different from any other tree, for it has been hidden away for years, I'm sure," said Charity.

They did not see Charlie for some time after this. They heard that he was ill, and one day a letter came from him addressed to "My Wife and Crew."

The little girls opened it with great delight. It was very short.

"This is to tell you that youre Captin lies dangirosly wunded, and his sickness is suvere. His next voyage will not take plaice, and when he gets better Ben is to come to him to delever messages to his wife and to Bolt.

"Charles, Captain of the 'Success.'"

Faith was Ben. She wondered why she was especially invited. Charity tossed her head.

"He knows he can do what he likes with Faith. I expect none of us will be able to go with him now, for Aunt Alice said we were to begin lessons. This new governess, Miss Vale, is coming next Monday."

"Well, anyhow," said Hope, "I'm glad it isn't school, and Aunt Alice says she will be very nice."

"I must answer his letter," said Faith.

But she was not very fond of letter-writing and put it off. She left Charity and Hope playing in the orchard that afternoon and went off to visit her friend the shepherd. There was nothing she enjoyed so much as creeping into his little cottage and sitting on a small stool in the chimney corner with the old man. Sandy would come and rest his nose in her lap, and she and Timothy found plenty to say to each other. She told him all about Charlie, and the raft and the Pirate.

"'Tis a pity the little laddie enjoys such poor health," said Timothy to her. "The doctor be such a hearty man, but there—the Lord have a way of His Own with each o' us, and 'tis ordained for him to be weakly. I often sits and thinks o' strength. 'Tis misused in the body, and if so be the soul is strong, 'tisn't so much odds about the body!"

"I wonder how strong my soul is," said Faith. "I'm not very strong in my body, Granny says. Can I make my soul strong, Timothy?"

"Ask the Comforter," said the old man. "He'll strengthen the weak. We are told 'He helpeth our infirmities.'"

"What do infirmities mean?"

"Our weakness and ailments, surely. The Book says, 'We can be strengthened with might in the inner man' by Him."

"Is our inner man our souls?" asked Faith.

"I suppose I have an inner woman—I'm not a man."

"'Tis just a figure o' speech. 'Tis your little soul you want to be made strong."

"I like the Comforter very much," said Faith softly and reverently; "He came and comforted me this morning, Timothy. Aunt Alice scolded me because she told us not to leave the front door open, there was such a wind. And Hope left it open; she came out last, and the wind knocked a china vase off the table, and broke it, and Aunt Alice was very angry and scolded me, because she thought I'd gone out last. And I went away and cried, and then I distinctly felt the Comforter near me, and I asked Him to comfort me. I almost felt He took me in His Arms. He was so close. And I kept quite still, and then I couldn't be sorry any more, for I knew He knew I hadn't done it. He was so kind!"

Faith heaved a sigh of happiness, and Timothy nodded his head.

"'Tis just so!" he said simply.

And then they began to talk about Sandy and the sheep, and when she left the cottage, Faith's little face was radiant.

"I feel when I'm talking to you," she said as she bade the old man farewell, "that I'm getting happier every minute. I shan't be able to come and see you so often when we do lessons, but I'll come whenever I can!"

Charity and Hope could not understand her friendship with the old man. But Faith paid no heed to them. She was a quiet, old-fashioned child, and loved to go her own way without any interference of other people.

CHAPTER VI
CHARLIE STILL IN COMMAND

MISS VALE arrived on Monday, and the little girls fell in love with her. She was very pretty, with bright, dark eyes, and a quick, cheerful manner. But they found she was very firm and strict in some things, and lessons could not be trifled with.

"I shall not give you any lessons you cannot prepare, and when I come I expect to find them done. If they are not, I shall conclude it is idleness that is the cause and will deal with it accordingly."

This sounded very alarming, but the children found that she was right, and that there was no excuse for their lessons not being learnt.

She came from nine o'clock to one, and they had an hour every afternoon in which they did what they called their "prep" for her.

Charity and Hope did everything together, Faith could not keep up with them. She was slow and persevering, but not very clever at books. Yet Miss Vale, if she had any preference, liked to teach her the best of the three, for her whole heart was in what she did, and she was extremely conscientious.

In a few days' time, Faith was allowed to go to see Charlie. His mother met her at the door.

"My boy did too much with you that day. He has been in bed ever since. His father says there must be no voyages down the stream for a long time to come, so don't encourage him to talk about it."

Faith was taken into the sitting-room, where Charlie lay on the couch, looking very white and frail, but he greeted her most cheerfully:

"Come on, Ben. Isn't it hard lines for me?"

"What's been the matter with you?" asked Faith in a sympathetic tone.

"Oh temperature; it's always that. My head nearly bursting and I'm hot as fire! But I'm all right now. What have you been doing?"

Faith gave an account of their days since last they met, and from being very bright Charlie's spirits sank, and he began to talk most gloomily.

"It's no use my trying to do anything like other fellows. If God had made me a girl, I shouldn't have minded half so much, but boys are meant to be strong, and I think it's a shame I shouldn't be. I quite hate myself sometimes. If I was meant to be weak and ill, I oughtn't to have been born a boy. It was a big mistake."

"But," said Faith with rather a shocked look, "God borned you, and He can't make mistakes. And I don't see why girls should be ill and not boys. Besides, Charlie, if you aren't strong outside, you can be inside. I was talking with my friend Timothy about you. He said:"

"'It wasn't any odds about the body, it's the soul that really matters.'"

"Don't you like people with strong souls?"

"I don't know what they're like," Charlie said, staring at her.

Faith's eyes grew big and glowed with light as she replied:

"Oh, they're heroes!—Always smiling at difficult days and going straight on with their heads up, even if they're hurt. I've thought about them a lot. And I'm hoping the Comforter will make my soul grow big and strong. I should like never to cry when I'm hurt, and never grumble when things are horrid! And keep smiling even if the whole world turned against me and trampled me down!"

Faith spoke with such fervour that Charlie was much impressed.

She added:

"We all think you have a strong soul because you're so cheerful."

"Oh, I'm not!" said Charlie. "I've been beastly to Mother I'm so awfully disappointed that Dad won't let me go on the raft. It's the one thing I really enjoy! There's nothing else I can play at. It does seem a shame."

"We play lots of games," said Faith, "and we've no raft."

"No, but you are girls, and you can run about, and climb trees. I've had a miserable time shut up here all alone."

"I suppose," said Faith shyly, "you wouldn't like the Comforter to stay with you? I think you would feel better if He did. I don't know Him very well yet, but Timothy talks to me about Him. And I think it's so wonderful that He likes coming and living with boys and girls and making them happy and good and strong!"

"What do you mean?" asked Charlie.

"Timothy told me about Him first. If you're ill and unhappy, He would like to come to you and comfort you. That's why He's called the Comforter. Wherever He goes He comforts, and He does it perfectly, because, you know, He is God."

Faith's voice sank to an awed whisper.

"What a funny girl you are!" said Charlie. "You seemed as if you were talking about a real person!"

"But the Comforter is real."

"Well, a real person is somebody you can see."

"If you can't see Him, you can hear Him," said Faith gravely. "There are lots of real things we can't see. The wind—"

"Oh, I know, but you're preaching a sermon."

"Am I?"

Faith subsided into silence. Presently she said:

"Then I can't tell you how to be happy and comforted, if you won't believe what Timothy says."

"Can you find out this puzzle?"

Charlie would have no more serious talk; and produced a little puzzle box with a padlock which opened itself in a wonderful way; Faith was interested at once. She paid him quite a long visit, and when the time came for her to go, Charlie produced two packets which he charged her to give to the wife and to Bolt.

"They're my wishes," he said. "You signed on to do what I told you for a year, and I'm still in command, though I'm ill!"

"Aye, sir, aye!" said Faith, saluting him in best style.

Then she went home, and Charity and Hope opened their packets eagerly.

There was a great deal of paper but not much writing. Charity's was as follows:

"Captain Charles sends greetings to his wife. He wishes her to find the Pirate's Haunt, and let me know his house and his riteful name. She must make the journey by land, but she must not fale to do it. For a lot hangs on the Finding! And she must rite the name in sekrecy and seal her letter with a red seal and send it through the post. And if she does not keep it sekret death will o'ertake her.

"(Signed) CAPTAIN CHARLES."

Hope opened hers and found a strange map, drawn in red ink by Charlie. This was the letter accompanying it.

"Captain Charles to his humble and devotted servant Bolt. I charge you to studey this map, and to find on your walks the place that is called Boggy Glen. There is a wonderful herbe therein, called Wild peppermint, whichesame will releave the Captain of his mortal sicknes, and is to be sent to me in a sealed letter by poste with no derlay.

"(Signed) CAPTAIN CHARLES."

"What fun!" cried Hope. "You and me, Charity, will have to be busy!"

"And he's given me nothing to do," said Faith, feeling aggrieved; "nothing at all."

"You're his messenger," said Charity, "you must take back answers to these notes. A King's messenger is most important, and so is a Captain's messenger."

Faith's face brightened. She took back two notes the next day to the doctor's house, but did not see Charlie. These were the notes:

"MY DEAR HUSBAND,

"I'm sorry you're sick, but I'll find the Pirate in a jiffy. I wish you had told me to hang him or something difficult like that, but after all I don't want him hanged, because he was very kind. I mustn't let him know of course. I'll criep about like a spy and follow his tracks. I think I've already found out his name. But I'll write it hidden in a sentence and you'll have to find it out. Good-bye and good luck.

"Your sooperior WIFE."

"MY DEAR CAPTAIN,

"I will find the heeling herb, no fear about that! And I'll make a potion of it to be swallowed at midnight in the dark. And you will rise up early a hale and harty man. So three cheers for our Captain and his crew.

"Yours as signed, BOLT."

Faith had these letters read aloud to her and she thought them wonderfully clever.

The very next day, Charity and Hope set off on their different quests. Faith wandered out alone. She called at Timothy's cottage, but he was out; and then she rambled on through some fields, and made her way along a strange lane, which had banks of primroses on each side. Presently she saw a hole through the hedge; she crept through, and then she started, for two men were talking together. They were standing by a rick of hay, and she heard one man say with passion in his tone:

"I tell you, Fielding, I'm so dead sick of rotting here like a vegetable, when I might be up and doing with the rest of the working world, that at times I feel inclined to make a bolt for it!"

"It's hard lines," murmured the other man, and then the two separated.

One went on across the field, the other turned and faced Faith, and she saw it was the Pirate. Just for a moment he looked as if he were going to pass her without speaking, and his brows were knitted so fiercely, and his face so gloomy, that Faith was frightened. He stood still, as he saw her shrinking into the hedge, and then his brow cleared.

"Why, it's one of the treasure seekers, isn't it?" he said in his pleasant voice.

Then Faith held out her small hand.

"I'm so glad you will speak to me," she said, "I should have been so disappointed, if you hadn't."

"Would you? And what are you doing alone here?"

"Just walking about and trying to amuse myself," answered Faith. "Charity and Hope have gone off to do errands for Charlie, but I've none to do."

For a moment she was tempted to tell him that Charity was looking for him, then she remembered that Charlie said it was to be kept a secret, so she shut her lips determinedly.

"Well, I'm an idle person too. We'll take a walk together, I want to go to Dapperton Bridge to see if there's a chance of any salmon there. Will you come with me?"

"Is it very far? I should love to."

"No, it is only half a mile further on."

He took hold of her hand, and chatted about different things till they came to the bridge; then he leant his arms on it, and as he gazed at the river flowing beneath, his face became gloomy again, and absorbed. Faith stood by his side and watched him, then she put her little hand softly on his arm.

"Are you very unhappy?" she asked.

He started, but did not look at her; his eyes were on the rushing water.

"I am not exactly happy, child," he said, slowly; "my life is distasteful. I'm a discontented grumbler, that's what I am. How did you find it out?"

"I heard you speak to that other man," said Faith, truthfully. "You said you were sick of it or something like it."

"So I did. Little pitchers have long ears they say, but it's true."

They were silent for a moment or two.

"Do you know a friend of mine called Timothy Bendall?" asked Faith suddenly.

"I'm afraid I haven't that pleasure."

"He's an old man, a shepherd who has a cottage all his own, and he lets me come in and talk to him. He's told me how all the unhappy people in the world can get happy, every one of them."

The young man gave a short laugh.

"And what is the wonderful recipe? How is it done?"

Faith looked up at him with shining eyes.

"They get to know the Comforter, and fancy! I didn't know He was in the world. Nobody ever talks about Him. Timothy says He loves unhappy people. It's what He keeps in the world for, instead of living in heaven, just to comfort them and make them happy. I suppose you know Him, don't you?"

"What an old-fashioned mite you are! I didn't know children thought about such things—they're never unhappy."

"Oh, we are, we are," said Faith eagerly. "Charlie is miserable because he's ill, and can't go any more on his raft, and we cry often and often. I haven't cried so much lately, because I've asked the Comforter to come and live with me. You can't cry very well when you feel Him quite close to you. I think you'd find He would make you very happy. If you went to Timothy, he would tell you all about Him. He reads bits of the Bible out to me. The Comforter is really God, you know. He came into the world when Jesus went out of it. Jesus sent him, so that nobody should feel sad."

"Go on," said the young man with a smile; "tell me more. You're quite a little preacher."

And then Faith got scarlet in her cheeks and stopped speaking.

"Charlie said I preached a sermon," she murmured. "I don't mean to do it, but it's so new to me, I like talking about it to people. Charity and Hope laugh at me, but they're hardly ever unhappy for long. I won't say any more. Have you seen any fish yet?"

"I like listening to you. Go on talking about this Comforter."

But Faith would say no more.

He did not press her, and presently the sight of a big fish rising with a splash seized her attention.

Then the Pirate began telling Faith about some wonderful salmon he had caught. He told her his name, which was the same as the children had heard—Fred Cardwell. He also told her about his poor sick father.

"Now, if he could believe in this Comforter you talk about, it would be a good thing for himself and every one else. Do you think you could come up one day and talk to him about it?"

"Timothy would," said Faith doubtfully; "I should be afraid to."

"But you weren't afraid of me, and my father is only a poor old sick man who hates his life, and makes everyone who comes near him as miserable as he is."

"Couldn't you tell him better than me?" said Faith, shyly.

"I'm sure I couldn't. Will you come to tea one day—you and your sisters—and play in an untidy old garden? Would you like to?"

"Oh, we should love it! We adore going out to tea, and everybody is so kind here. And we love seeing new gardens. Nobody had gardens in London."

"All right. One day I'll drive over for the three of you. Would the Captain like to come too?"

"He's ill now. Oh, how kind you are!"

Faith danced softly up and down on her toes. Then her friend walked back to the village with her and she ran home and told Granny all about her meeting.

Granny was amused.

"You children seem making friends with everybody," she said. "But don't set your heart upon people's promises. They often go their way and forget. A grown-up man does not often care to entertain children."

When Charity and Hope came home they had as much to tell Faith as she had to tell them.

Hope had found the wild peppermint in the right place. She had been studying her map as she walked along the road, and the old Rector came up and told her at once how she could find Boggy Glen. It was over some fields behind a pine wood. Charity had not been so fortunate, but the post office woman had told her that the Towers was the name of Mr. Cardwell's place, and a carrier's cart passed it every Wednesday.

"If only Miss Vale would give us a holiday, I could go," said Charity, "but she won't. And I'm not quite sure that the Pirate is Mr. Cardwell."

"But I'm sure," cried Faith delightedly, "because I've been talking to him, and we're all going to his house to tea very soon."

Then she told her story, and Charity was not best pleased.

"You've been doing what I ought to have done," she said. "You'd no business to go and speak to him. You ought to have come off and told me where he was."

"But I didn't know where to find you," said Faith.

Charity sniffed.

"It's not secret at all if you know all about it," she said. "You've spoiled the whole thing!"

She walked out of the room as she spoke, and banged the door behind her.

Faith felt inclined to cry, but Hope told her that Charity had come home tired and cross, and that she didn't mean what she said, and when the sisters met at tea Charity was her bright self again, and quite interested about writing her sealed letter to the captain.

"I shall tell him I have gained the information from a trustworthy person, but I shan't tell him it's you," she said.

Faith brightened up.

"And you did hear about him first, didn't you?" she cried.

Charity nodded.

"It will be fun if we go to tea with him properly. Mrs. Budd, at the post office, told me it was a beautiful house, but that old Mr. Cardwell led his son a dog's life. I wonder what that means?"

No one could enlighten her.

After tea, Charity wrote her letter, and Hope was very busy soaking her mint in hot water, and pouring it into a bottle which she begged from her aunt. She managed to put a drop or two of vinegar in it and some salt, so she assured her sisters it was quite as nasty as it ought to be. And then there was a great fuss sealing the packages up. Granny found an odd bit of sealing wax she lent them. Charity read her sentence out proudly to her sisters in which the Pirate's name was buried. It was this:

"First read end down. Cut all right dates with easy little letters."

And she added below: "Follow this advice and you will find what you want."

Faith could not understand it at all, until Charity showed that the first letters of each word spelt his name, and then she thought it wonderfully clever and wondered if Charlie would discover it quickly.

She took the packages off that same evening, but only left them at the door for him, as Granny said she was not to stay, for bed-time was close at hand.

And all three children went to bed very satisfied with their day's work.

CHAPTER VII
THE PIRATE'S HOME

CHARLIE was delighted with his packages and wrote a little note thanking them, but he was not allowed out of his bedroom yet, and for the time the little girls had to be content to play without him.

Sir George arrived one morning, wanting to carry off the children to lunch with his wife, but Miss Vale was very stern and would not let lessons be interfered with. So he deferred his invitation to the afternoon, and then they went to tea with Lady Melville instead. As before, Charity and Hope went off with Sir George to see his books and horses, and Faith stayed to talk to Lady Melville. Of course she told her of their new friend, the Pirate, and Lady Melville knew all about him.

"I wish he would come and see us oftener; but he is rather unsociable, and he does not lead a natural life. He is a devoted son, but a man ought not to be a sick nurse; that is a woman's vocation."

Then Lady Melville smiled at Faith's puzzled face.

"I always forget I am talking to a child," she said. "You seem like a grown-up person sometimes, little Faith."

"I don't feel like one," said Faith, smiling. "Is old Mr. Cardwell very dreadful? Everybody says he is. If we go to tea there, shall we have to see him?"

"I don't think you will. He is the last person in the world to have children about him. Poor old man! He has always rebelled against his fate, and as he gets older seems to grow more bitter and angry. He used to hunt a great deal, but he has been stretched helpless on a bed for nearly ten years, and I don't think he is able to raise his hand to his mouth. It is very, very sad, and no one seems able to help him."

Faith was silent, but her thoughts were busy.

Then Lady Melville began to talk about Charlie Evans. He was a more cheerful subject of conversation, and Faith chattered away, telling of all their games. She was quite sorry when her sisters came back into the drawing-room. When they were present, Faith grew silent.

They had a very nice tea, and as they were going away, Lady Melville said:

"My boys come home next week for the Easter holidays. I wish they were not quite so big, for they would be better companions for you, but we must try and get some young people in the neighbourhood together one day and then you must all come too."

As the little girls walked home, Charity said:

"Sir George told me that in the summer holidays, there would be picnics, and garden parties, and all kinds of nice things, but he says his boys don't do much but fish when they come home now. I think we have come to a lovely place to live. We never had such treats in London."

"We sometimes went out to tea," said Hope; "but it makes such a difference when there are big gardens to play in."

Faith skipped gaily along the road.

"I like going out to tea anywhere," she said; "I like having tea with Timothy, and he has no garden."

"I believe I know why we enjoy ourselves better in the country," said Charity thoughtfully. "Grownup people are kinder to us here. They have time to talk to us, and they have no time in London. They are always so busy there, and in such a rush!"

Hope nodded.

"Yes, when Aunt Alice's friends came to see her they always said, 'I've no time to stay, I don't know how to get through!' Why do people rush about so in London?"

"They always shop so much," said Charity; "and there are no shops here; and then I suppose the crowds of people make a difference, they have so many friends to see."

"Well," said Faith, "we have friends here. I have Timothy, and Charlie, and Sir George and Lady Melville, and the Pirate, that's five, and perhaps we may have more."

"Timothy doesn't count," said Charity scornfully; "and the Pirate is almost a stranger. We may never see him again."

"He is going to have us to tea," said Faith eagerly.

But Charity tossed her head unbelievingly.

"He has forgotten all about it," she said.

Faith knew better, and three days after, as they were doing their lessons in the tiny best parlour which had been turned into their schoolroom, they saw through the window, the Pirate ride up to the gate on a big brown horse. Aunt Alice went out to speak to him, and she had quite a long conversation at the gate.

Miss Vale, seeing how this distracted her pupils' attention from their lessons, and how each of the little girls would stare out of the window, promptly stepped across the room and drew down the blind. Charity was the only one who was brave enough to offer an objection:

"You should control your curiosity," said Miss Vale cheerfully. "You are very poor things, if you always let that get the better of you. And your eyes must be on your lesson books, don't let them run off anywhere else. Whilst you are little, you must learn to be masters of your members. Do you understand what I mean?"

The children shook their heads.

"Your eyes must not look away from what you are doing. If your brain insists that they do not, you are the master of your members, and the same with your hands and your feet. Charity need not let her feet kick the legs of her chair when she is impatient, nor need Hope bite her finger nails, nor Faith slip her feet in and out of her shoes. Don't say, 'I can't help it,' for that is letting your hands and feet manage you, instead of you managing them!"

Miss Vale had successfully captured their attention now. It was a new idea to all of them, that they had to manage their hands and feet as well as their eyes and the other parts of their body.

Lessons went on very quietly after that, but when Miss Vale had gone, they rushed off to find their Aunt Alice.

"Well," she said, "I expect you have guessed already. Mr. Cardwell is coming to-morrow to drive you over to the Towers to spend the afternoon."

"Our dear Pirate, how lovely!" exclaimed Charity.

Faith got pink with pleasure.

"All of us are to go?" questioned Hope.

"Yes. I think it is remarkably good of him to be troubled with you," said Aunt Alice laughing.

The next afternoon at three o'clock a very high and smart dogcart stopped at the gate, and the children walked out most importantly to meet it.

"If only Mrs. Cox could see us!" said Hope.

They packed themselves in with glee.

"We don't feel a bit frightened of going with you now," said Charity; "but we were rather nervous the other day, when you played pirate and pretended you were going to take us prisoners. Even when you said you'd lead us to the treasure, we suspected treachery."

"You are quite sure I'm to be trusted now?"

"Oh, yes, because you've seen Aunt Alice!"

They had the most delightful drive, and the Pirate was most amusing.

"You seem to understand very well," said Hope, when he had been condoling with them about the unhappiness of monotony.

"Ah," he said, "I remember when I was a boy how I loved all unexpected events, I didn't care how grown-up people were inconvenienced. If a cistern burst, and the water came pouring downstairs, if the wind blew a tree down and smashed an open casement window, if a cook ran off, and left us without any dinner, or any other domestic disaster came upon us, how delighted and excited I was!"

"Yes," chuckled Charity. "I think disasters are more exciting than pleasures. I almost wish we could have some at the Cottage. Mrs. Cox used to have a lot happen to her, but we never did!"

"Would you like to be tossed by a furious bull? We have one in a field by himself, he's a bad-tempered brute."

"Oh, no," cried Faith. "I don't like disasters at all; we have come out to enjoy ourselves. It's when we're very dull, we wish for accidents and things of that sort."

"I'll do my best to prevent you feeling dull," the Pirate said.

The Towers was a bigger house than Sir George's, but the children all agreed it was a gloomy looking place. The shrubberies and evergreen oaks round it overshadowed it, ivy crept up the stone walls, but no climbing roses or jessamine or any sweet scented creeper. In front of the house was a tiled garden with fountains and stone vases; the weeds grew apace everywhere, and there were only flowering shrubs, no bright flower beds.

Still it was lovely to explore, there were so many winding paths and walled gardens.

For an hour the little girls were absolutely happy, rambling about the grounds and seeing all that the Pirate could show them. Then he took them into the house, through a big stone hall, into a very comfortable smoking-room, where, he told them, he always lived, and where tea was now laid out on a square table.

"What a lot of rooms you have," said Charity; "don't you use them all?"

"No, most of them are shut up. It's a barrack of a place, and wants a large family to occupy it."

"You've got too big a house," said Hope thoughtfully, "and we have too little a one. We're dreadfully crowded. We have to be so tidy, that it takes up all our time putting our things away!"

"I wish I could cut off a slice of this house and stick it on to yours," said the Pirate.

"Wouldn't it be fun if you could!" said Charity. "I see you've a lot of books but not so many as Sir George. I mean to have a house full of books when I grow up; a very big house I shall have, and an enormous library!"

They chattered on and made a very good tea; in fact, there were so many biscuits and cakes that Charity said she did not consider it a war tea. When it was over, the Pirate took Charity and Hope upstairs to a big picture gallery. He left them there looking at the pictures, whilst he asked Faith to follow him along a wide passage to a room at the end of it.

"Now," he said, "come in and see my father. Remember he is a poor sick old gentleman, and talk to him as you did to me the other day, and tell him how he can be happy."

Faith shrank back, then fighting with her fears she took hold of the Pirate's hand.

"I'm very afraid," she said, "and p'raps he won't like to see me. And I can't talk to him like I do to you."

"Never mind, just talk to him about anything."

And then the Pirate opened the door of a large sunny room; there were four big windows in a row, and drawn up to one of them, which was wide open, was a big couch. The invalid was lying on it, but he did not turn his head when they, came in.

An elderly man-servant was standing by his couch; he was just taking away a small tray of tea which stood on a table by the side of it, and old Mr. Cardwell was thundering out:

"You clumsy fool! Can't you do your duties without shaking the whole room with your heavy tread? And pull down the blind—that confounded sun is—"

He stopped short, for he had caught sight of Faith. She was promptly introduced:

"A little friend of mine, father, whom I am going to leave with you for a short time."

Without waiting for a response, the Pirate hurried away, the servant following him as quickly as he could.

Faith found herself standing by the couch, facing an angry old man.

Faith's greatest friends always said her extreme gentleness was her chief attraction. With her small heart beating violently, she had self-control enough to place her soft little hand on the old helpless wrinkled hand that was restlessly moving to and fro.

"I hope I shan't disturb you," she said.

Old Mr. Cardwell looked at her tiny face with its earnest eyes, and pointed chin, and sensitive little mouth, and was speechless.

Her soft lisping voice, for most of Faith's "s's" sounded like "th's," and her still softer touch made him say with a short laugh:

"Disturb me! You've alighted in my room like a butterfly or moth—a little grey moth, that's what you are!"

Faith wore a grey hat and coat, and the simile was apt.

"Now, what the d—ahem!—dickens, does Fred mean by landing you here and leaving you here?"

Faith did not speak.

"Are you tongue tied, child?"

"No, I'm—a little afraid of you—not very much, for you look a little like my dearest friend."

"And who is he?"

"Timothy his name is. He isn't ill like you, but he has a beard, and his eyes are blue. I think I came to see you to tell you about him."

"Sit down in that chair, little Miss Moth. Now tell me about yourself, not about this old bearded Timothy."

Faith smiled all over her face.

"I do love it when people give me names. Sir George calls me Curly, and Charlie calls me Ben. My real name is Faith. Will you always call me Miss Moth?"

"Is there going to be an always? Have you come into my house prepared to take root and stay?"

"Oh, no, we're going home very soon, we've come to tea with the Pirate. May I tell you?"

So the whole story was poured out, and the lonely, irritable old man listened, and felt a faint interest in the little speaker.

"Well," he said, when she had finished, "I'm a miserable old man, a living, helpless log; and Fred, who poses to you children as a gallant pirate, is my gaoler, and he hates his job and I don't wonder at it!"

Faith looked at him with her great eyes. Then she bent forward eagerly:

"Why don't you have Somebody I know come and live with you? He would make you so very happy."

"Happy! That's a strange word to use, Miss Moth."

"Oh, it's all true!"

Faith threw off her shyness, she began to speak eagerly:

"I've only been hearing about Him lately. Timothy told me. Mrs. Cox used to say the world was an unhappy place—a weary world she called it; she said we were born to trouble—but she didn't know what I do. Nobody, not a single person, need be unhappy, they've only got to send for the Comforter. He's waiting, He wants to comfort, He goes all over the world finding out the sad.

"Hasn't He ever come to you? It's what He stays in the world for. Jesus sent Him when He went away from us. Do you know about Him? You couldn't possibly be unhappy if you have Him staying with you. Timothy told me thousands of people have died in agonies of pain—they were burnt alive, lots of them—and they only smiled because the Comforter put His Arms round them and held them tight. It's what I ask Him to do to me, to hold me so tight that I only feel Him and nothing else. He wipes away tears, and tells us it is all right, and He knows and He loves us. And I'm getting to love Him so much since I've known about Him. It's Timothy who teaches me. Oh, I wish you could hear how he tells about it. He says if anybody is sick the Comforter is ready to go to them at once."

She stopped. Old Mr. Cardwell gazed at her as if he had never seen or heard a child talk before.

"Well, I'm dashed!" he said. "There, that's a harmless exclamation! Where on earth do you get your gift of eloquence from? You little insignificant grey moth, talking of personalities that doctors of divinity are chary of mentioning! So you think I could be made content and happy. Will you take me in hand?"

Faith looked puzzled.

"Go on," he said, "talk away. I like to hear you. Perhaps you had better describe this wonderful Timothy to me. Is he a spirit, or is he flesh and blood?"

"Timothy is a shepherd. He has a dog and a little cottage. He lives close to us. I sit on a stool by his fire, and he sits in a big wooden chair and he smokes a pipe—oh, I wish you knew Timothy. Would you like him to come and see you?"

"Indeed I would not!"

There was a grim smile on the invalid's lips, the first that had lingered there for many a long day.

Half an hour later the Pirate came into the room, and found Faith with a happy face chattering to his father as if she had known him all her life.

He told her the trap was at the door, and Faith rose at once and shook hands with the invalid.

"Good-bye, and thank you for talking to me," she said.

Mr. Cardwell looked at his son.

"I congratulate you on your discovery," he said. "She can come again if she likes. I'll never shut my door upon her."

The Pirate knew how many times his father's door had been shut upon unwelcome visitors, and he took Faith away with a glad heart.

Then the children were driven home, and chattered all the evening to their Granny and Aunt, telling of all that they had seen and done.

CHAPTER VIII
CHARITY PLAYS TRUANT

THE very next day the three little girls met Lionel and Fairfax Melville at the village shop.

Charity was shopping for her aunt, and she was doing it with her most important air. Hope and Faith were outside the door looking in at the window, and wondering if it would be very wicked in war-time to buy two pennyworth of sweets. Suddenly two cyclists dashed up and dismounted. They were boys of fourteen and fifteen, and had come to the shop to buy some machine oil. They did not notice Faith and Hope, but stared at Charity, and then the elder, Lionel, who had a very frank, easy way with him, said:

"I believe you're Carrots, aren't you? The Pater calls you that."

"Yes," said Charity beaming, "and you're Lionel and Fairfax. We've seen your pictures."

She had finished her shopping, and did not like to linger, but as she was going out she said:

"If we were boys, we could chum up together, but we're girls."

"Yes," said Lionel, with an awkward laugh; "I suppose you don't fish? Girls never do."

"We could learn," said Charity. "Good-bye!"

Then she walked out of the shop; and wished harder than ever that she was a boy.

"They're too big for us," said Hope dejectedly. "Charlie is more our sort. I wish he would make haste and get well."

They did not see the boys again for some days, and then Charity met with a nasty accident, and Fairfax came to her aid. She was trying to get some marshmallows that grew by the side of the river, and in stretching out for them, she fell in. Happily a tree stretched over the water, and she managed to get hold of a branch, and cling on to it, whilst she called wildly for help. Fairfax and Lionel were fishing a short distance off, and Fairfax came up and soon pulled her up to the bank again.

"What a little duffer to fall in!" he said.

Charity stood and shivered in her wet clothes, but resented his tone.

"Anybody may have an accident," she said loftily.

"Run home and change your clothes," said Fairfax.

Charity walked away trying to appear dignified, but she was very near tears.

"I'll race you," said Fairfax. "Girls ought to be able to run."

Charity prided herself upon her swiftness. Dignity was forgotten. She sped away, and Fairfax could not outdistance her.

"I say, you can leg it!" he said.

When Charity arrived at the Cottage she stopped, and turned to him quite graciously, though she could hardly speak from breathlessness.

"Thank you for pilling me out," she said. "You're the one that likes books, aren't you?" Fairfax nodded.

"And you're the one who has been reading some of my books in the library," he said, "and my Greek legend book is missing."

"Sir George said I could borrow it. Do you mind?"

He laughed.

"Of course I don't, if you take care of it. We're going to take our lunch out to-morrow, we're walking out to the keeper's cottage the other side of our coverts. It's at the top of Hobbs Hill, it's A1 there. Like to come? Can you do three miles there and three back?"

"Oh, I could easy! Oh, how I should like to come, but we do lessons! And we aren't having holidays like you."

Charity's face fell.

"Take a day off! Play truant! Here's somebody! I'm off!"

He scampered back as Aunt Alice came to the gate. She was so concerned at Charity's wet state that she could not listen to her account of her misfortune. She popped her in bed and gave her a hot drink, and then Hope and Faith came upstairs to hear all about it.

Charity did not like staying in bed and protested loudly; then Aunt Alice scolded her, and said she deserved a punishment for being so careless, and Charity pursed up her mouth in a naughty way, and said:

"Then I shall do it to-morrow."

Hope asked her what she should do, but she would not say.

The next morning they settled down to lessons as usual. From nine to ten they worked steadily, and then Miss Vale took Hope to her music lesson. There was a small piano in the corner of the room. Charity and Faith were working at their arithmetic whilst the music was going on.

Presently Charity slipped out of the room. Nobody noticed her absence or thought it strange till Faith happened to hear the click of the garden gate, and looking out, saw Charity in her coat and hat running away from the cottage as fast as she could. She stared out as if she could not believe her eyes. What was Charity doing? Then she tried to bring her attention back to her sum, but it was quite impossible.

When Miss Vale left the piano and came back, she scolded her sharply for her idleness.

"You have only done one tiny sum this whole half-hour! For shame, Faith!"

Faith hung her head.

"I couldn't seem to think it out," she said.

"Where is Charity? I did not hear her leave the room."

Faith made no reply. After waiting a little, Miss Vale went to the door and called. There was no answer. Aunt Alice came out of the kitchen, and said she had not seen her. Hope was sent upstairs to look for her, and came back to say she was nowhere in the house. Faith's cheeks were burning, and there was such a troubled look in her eyes that Miss Vale noticed it.

"You know where she is, Faith. Tell me."

Faith wriggled in her seat. It was a point of honour with the sisters never to tell tales of each other.

"I don't know where she is now, Miss Vale, I really don't," Faith murmured at last.

"Tell me what you know about her."

Faith shook her head.

"She couldn't tell tales, Miss Vale," said Hope, "'specially if Charity's doing something she oughtn't. It's quite exciting! I do wonder where she is?"

"I'm afraid, Faith, you must tell me what you know," said Miss Vale.

And then Faith began to cry.

"I don't know anything," she sobbed; "I only saw her from the window going out at the gate."

She felt she had betrayed her sister most meanly, but Miss Vale had such a determined way with her, that she was compelled to tell the truth.

It all seemed strange and perplexing.

Then Miss Vale said lessons must continue, and for the rest of the morning she had two pupils with very wandering thoughts and divided attention.

When lessons hours were over, Charity was still absent. Miss Vale went home, and the children had their dinner. Granny was anxious, and Aunt Alice cross.

"I can't conceive how she dared behave so," Aunt Alice said. "She has never before gone off like this."

Then Hope suddenly guessed.

"I believe Fairfax Melville asked her to go out with him to-day," she said. "He pulled her out of the water, you know. Charity told him she couldn't go because of lessons. I shouldn't wonder if she has done it."

"It she has, she will have to be severely punished," said Aunt Alice.

But she and Granny seemed relieved by this possibility.

Faith and Hope played with their dolls in the orchard in the afternoon, but they talked a great deal about Charity.

"Isn't she daring?" said Hope. "I wish children could do those kind of things without getting punished. It's the afterwards that's so dreadful!"

But she spoke in admiring tones, and could not understand why Faith was so distressed about it.

"She has only played truant like children do in books, only it's easier to manage if you go to school."

"But think, when she walks in and has to meet Granny and Aunt Alice," said Faith. "Why, I should be ready to die, if I had to do it."

"Oh, Charity isn't so soft as you. Perhaps she'll get Sir George to bring her back, and then Granny won't be so angry."

"Granny is only sorry, not angry," said Faith; "but Aunt Alice is very angry indeed. She said to Granny that she deserved a whipping."

Hope and Faith looked at each other with awed eyes. The afternoon seemed long to them. Tea-time came and passed, still no Charity. At last, at half-past seven, just as Faith was being sent to bed, the truant arrived. She walked up to the door with firm step and head lifted high, but there was a nervous look in her eyes, and she was pale and was biting her lips, a trick which was her custom when perturbed.

Aunt Alice met her in the passage.

"Well, Charity, what is the meaning of this?"

"I only missed two hours' lessons," said Charity, trying to speak grandly; "and I thought I'd make them up to-morrow. I knew it was no good asking, but I've been spending the day out with Lionel and Fairfax, and—" here she paused, then rushed the words breathlessly and defiantly—"I've had a glorious time!"

This was no repentant sinner.

Aunt Alice marched her upstairs to her own bedroom, and she was closeted there with her a good half-hour.

Faith and Hope were both in bed when Charity came into the room. She had been crying. Her sisters felt sorry for her, but intensely curious. They had hardly ever seen her cry, and they felt that they would not shame her by showing her that they saw it, so they pretended to be asleep and covered their heads over with the bedclothes, leaving a little hole to peep out of, and watch her secretly.

Charity soon discovered this. She faced them boldly.

"You needn't peep at me like that! I'm not going to speak to you or tell you anything at all, so you can just go to sleep."

Then Hope threw back the bedclothes.

"We're so sorry for you, Charity."

"I hate your sorriness!"

Charity's tone was furious, and Hope dared say no more. Very soon she and Faith were fast asleep, but Charity lay awake, and sobbed her heart out. Some time later, the door of the children's room opened very softly. It was Granny. She came to Charity's bed, shielding her lighted candle with her hand, so that the rays should not disturb the sleeping children.

Charity lay very still and quiet, with closed eyes, feigning sleep, but Granny saw the swollen, reddened eyelids.

"Poor little soul!" she murmured, and then she knelt down by the bedside and bowed her head in prayer. Her whispered words were heard distinctly by Charity.

"Oh, Loving Father, pity and forgive, and save this dear child from the evils of self-will and waywardness. May her strong character be for good and not for evil, and teach us how to train her for her Saviour's sake. Amen."

Then there was a convulsive movement in the small bed, and Charity's arms were round Granny's neck.

"I'm awake, and I'm sorry and miserable, Granny, and I never will behave so wickedly again. Don't leave off loving me. Aunt Alice has. She's simply furious!"

"No, no, my darling, your Aunt is vexed. She has a right to be, but she has forgiven you already."

"But I'm to be punished to-morrow."

"To stamp it upon your memory," said Granny; then she kissed Charity very lovingly:

"Tell God what you have told me, my child, and go to sleep. You have a fresh day to begin to-morrow, and wake up good."

Then Granny went away. She never said much to the children, but she knew that Aunt Alice's words to her niece had been many and severe, and she did not wish to add to them.

It was a very subdued Charity who came to lessons next morning. She apologised to Miss Vale for what she had done, and for the whole of that afternoon Charity sat in the schoolroom writing an imposition for her aunt. It was only one sentence she had to write over and over again, many hundreds of times.

"Self-will and independence, unless under authority, always lead to disaster. Charity Blair."

Her back ached, her fingers ached, and her head ached before she had finished, but Charity had learned her lesson, and she never played truant again.

She told Faith and Hope afterwards about her day, and though she joined the boys, and actually caught a fish with a rod which they lent her, and though she had talked and laughed with them and was as jolly as she could be, underneath all was the miserable feeling of having done wrong.

"It doesn't really pay," she said.

Later on the three little girls spent an afternoon at the Hall with some other boys and girls. Charlie was well enough to be out again, and he was there.

Faith felt sorry for him when he could not join the boys in a game of hockey, but his spirits were good, and Sir George took him and Faith to see a small museum of curiosities, which interested them greatly.

He gave them each a small Roman coin with a hole pierced through, and told them that it was used in the time when our Lord was in the Holy Land.

"Do you think," said Faith, "that it could possibly be that Jesus Christ had this in His own Hand. Could He, do you think?"

"I shouldn't like to say," said Sir George.

When Faith got home, she put her coin in a little box which she kept carefully locked, and every night she would open it and finger it lovingly.

Charity warned her against making an idol of it.

Faith asked how a piece of money could be an idol.

"Anything is an idol if you worship it, or love it better than God," said Charity, with her superior air.

"But I don't worship it, and I only love it because it might have belonged to Jesus."

"I think that's very irreverent," said Charity.

"If you don't love it more than you ought to do, will you give it to me?"

"Never, never! It's my very own."

Faith shut up her box hastily and pocketed the key. After that she only took it out and looked at it when she was quite alone.

Lionel and Fairfax soon went back to school, and Charlie began his lessons again.

Then one Saturday afternoon, just before three o'clock, the Pirate's high dogcart appeared in charge of a groom. A note was sent in, which demanded an answer, and it was addressed to "Little Miss Moth."

Faith's fingers trembled as she opened the envelope.

"Will little Miss Moth keep a lonely old man company this afternoon? If so, she must return in the trap.

"W. CARDWELL."

A very short note, but it sent the colour flying into Faith's cheeks and the light into her eyes.

"Oh, Granny, Aunt Alice, may I go?"

Permission was given. Charity and Hope were very disappointed that they were not asked too. They went out and talked to the groom whilst Faith was getting ready to go, and Hope stroked the bay mare's nose and talked affectionately to her. They were not quite so disappointed when they heard that the Pirate was in London.

"It wouldn't be much fun to sit and talk to an old man the whole time," said Hope.

"No," said Charity; "Faith is so funny; she likes talking to Timothy. So dull, I think."

Faith drove off with a radiant face, and she entered the invalid's room with the same expression.

"Ah!" said the old man. "You're glad to come, then? You don't look so perturbed as when you saw me first."

"I love coming," said Faith.

She settled herself down in a chair which was put in readiness for her by the old man's side, and she and he talked away about all kinds of things. Then very mysteriously Faith brought out of her pocket her precious little box.

"I want to show you something wonderful," she said, "I thought you might like to see it."

CHAPTER IX
FAITH'S OLD FRIEND

OLD Mr. Cardwell admired the coin, but was not quite so much impressed as Faith considered he ought to be. He rang the bell for his servant, and told him to bring a small cabinet. Then he asked for his bunch of keys, and he made Faith unlock it, and take out some old coins that he had collected.

"These are all B.C.," he said. "Hundreds of years before."

Faith looked at them, asked what "B.C." meant, and in her turn was not much impressed.

"I shouldn't care for them so much," she said. "It's only because this might—it might, you know—have lain in the Hand of Jesus."

"Oh, you little piece of superstition!" said the old man. "You ought to have been born an R.C. Then you would have believed anything."

"But I might be right," said Faith. "Nobody could make sure I'm not, and I like to think it, very, very much."

"Why are you so religious? Is it the way in your family? Children aren't as a rule. What makes you such a little sober-sides?"

Faith shook her curls.

"I can't tell you," she said, "but I don't feel sober when I come to see you. I feel I could dance for joy, and I don't think I'm religious—we're pretty naughty, as a rule."

Then she put her coin back carefully in its box.

"I think the children who lived in the Bible time when Jesus Christ went about their villages were the most fortunate children in the world."

There was a pause in their conversation.

Then her little face brightened.

"But I suppose we're fortunate, too, for we have the Comforter going about with us in the world now."

"Ah!" said old Mr. Cardwell, "I thought you would start that hare again. How's the old shepherd? Seen him lately?"

"Yes, one day last week. I met him in the road, taking his sheep to another field, and Sandy was with him. Timothy knows you. I asked him if he did. And he feels very sorry for our Pirate, because he wanted to go to the war, didn't he? And they wouldn't have him, because he had a bad heart?"

"That was the way of it. Bad luck has been in this house for twenty years—ever since I lost my wife."

"Did she die?" Faith asked with interest.

"Yes, caught a cold—and died after three days' illness. Everything went wrong after that."

"You must have felt just like the disciples did," said Faith thoughtfully.

The old man did not reply. A shadow had come across his face, but there was a softer look in his eyes as he thought about the wife he had adored.

"Me and Timothy sat down in a field together under a tree," went on Faith, "while he ate his dinner. He had some cold bacon and bread. It was very nice, I tasted it. And then he told me the story of the disciples. You see, it was simply awful for them when Jesus went away from them like your wife did! Shall I tell you what Timothy told me?"

"Oh, yes, tell me anything you like."

"You see, they thought all along Jesus wouldn't die. They wouldn't and couldn't believe it when He told them He was going away from them. And they hoped to the last He wouldn't die, and then He did. It was awful black and dark, and no good to live any more, they thought. Timothy said they'd always told Jesus all their troubles, and He had understood, and they'd loved Him so, and they'd followed and lived with Him, and when He was silent and dead their hearts nearly broke. Timothy says they felt what we feel when one we love best dies—you felt like that about your wife, didn't you? I almost wished when Timothy was talking that I had somebody I loved very much who died. But I did know a little girl at our school in London who died, and we cried a good deal, because she was in my class, and she came to tea once, and I was sorry after that I didn't let her have one of my dolls' hats. She asked for it, I remember!"

Faith paused for breath; her thoughts had flown away on another track. The invalid looked at her with some amusement in his eyes.

Then she returned to the subject of Timothy's conversation.

"Well, just before their hearts quite broke, Jesus rose out of his grave on Easter Sunday, and then they were most joyful again. And He often came and talked to them, but then came another dreadful disappointment. He went away from them for good and all, and never came back again. And He hasn't come yet, though He will one day."

Faith paused.

"Of course you know all this don't you? Because it's in the Bible, but Timothy makes it quite real when he tells it. Shall I go on—the best part is just coming—"

"Go on. I'm listening."

"Well, they were told by angels when Jesus went up to Heaven that the Comforter was coming to them, and they must just pray and wait for Him. And then one wonderful day they were all together, and there was a rushing mighty wind, and the Comforter came."

Faith's eyes were big now with delight and awe. She waved her small hands in the air in her excitement:

"He came right on them and into them, and they dried their tears and never cried again; and they found they could do anything they wanted now, and weren't afraid of the wicked Jews or of death, or any of the fearful things that come into the world to make us unhappy and sad. And then they began to see that what Jesus said was quite, quite true. The Comforter went about with them everywhere and kept them good and happy, and made them remember every single word Jesus had ever said to them. And they lived happy ever after till they died, and then the Comforter carried them up to heaven, and they've been there ever since. Isn't that a beautiful ending?"

Old Mr. Cardwell gazed at the child's shining face and was speechless for a minute, then he said:

"But you don't think that the same thing happens to us?"

"Timothy says it does, really it does. And everybody who feels when they've got their dear soldiers dying and leaving them that they can never be happy again, are making a little mistake. Because the Comforter is only too glad to come and make it up to them, and dry their tears and make them quite happy again. I asked Timothy if we all heard the wind when the Comforter came. He says He comes very gently now. But yesterday, all day, there was such a rushing wind round our cottage and in the orchard, that I wondered if the Comforter was coming to a whole lot of unhappy people all at once, like He did to the disciples. What do you think? Did He come to you when your wife died in a very soft way, or in a loud way?"

"He's never come near me at all," said the old man with a bitter smile.

Faith looked at him in a perplexed fashion.

"Well, then, I suppose He is waiting to be asked, like with me. I never asked Him to come to me before Timothy told me about Him. I really didn't understand. But I asked Him as soon as I could. And Timothy says He is with me. I s'pose—"

Faith stopped, and a slow, dreamy smile came upon her lips: "I s'pose whatever happens to me when I grow up and when I get quite old—if a earthquake shakes me, or Granny and Aunt Alice and Charity and Hope are all taken to Heaven first, and me left behind quite alone, and if the most awful things you can imagine would happen—I shall never, never be unhappy, because the Comforter will be drying my tears as fast as they come, and holding me in His Arms and loving me."

There was dead silence. A little breeze blew in at the open window, and then a red and brown butterfly flew in and alighted on the rug that covered the invalid's legs.

Childlike, Faith jumped up to look at it. Her grave talk was forgotten.

"I suppose a moth isn't as pretty as a butterfly is it? You will always call me Miss Moth, won't you? I do love it."

"Well, little Miss Moth, I'm much obliged for your dear little sermon. We'll have the rest of it another day."

The butterfly flew away, and Faith watched it alight on a rhododendron outside. Then she turned:

"Oh, dear, everybody tells me I give sermons! I don't mean to. And I'm not partickly fond of sermons myself, they're so long and dry. But I do love talking about the Comforter. Charity and Hope won't listen; they say they don't want any comfort at all. I s'pose if you're never unhappy you don't. But they do get miserable sometimes."

She stopped. Tea was being brought in, and she had the supreme joy of handling the silver teapot, and pouring out cups of tea for herself and the old man. She chattered away now of the Cottage, and of the village, and of all that she and her sisters meant to do in the summer holidays; and when the time came for her to go, she parted from her old friend with real regret.

But she was made happy by the invitation to come and spend every Saturday afternoon with him. And when she got home her tongue went fast. Charity told her that she would get sick and tired of the old invalid before long.

"It's only because he's new. After two or three weeks you'll feel quite dull, and won't want to go any more."

"I shall always want to go," said Faith emphatically; "he talks nearly as nice as Timothy, only different, but they both talk to me in a understanding way."

Charity laughed.

"It isn't very hard to understand you," she said.

Faith coloured and crept away with her feelings a little hurt. Hope came after her.

"Never mind, Faith. Let's come and put Rose and Violet to bed. They're up in the apple tree. Charity is always saying nasty things, but she doesn't mean them. But she says you're trying to get religious like the children in books. And that's priggy, you know!"

"I'm sure I don't mean to be," said Faith disconsolately.

But she cheered up when they were out in the sunny orchard; and the putting of the dolls to bed was a serious business, and occupied her time and thoughts. Faith had been going to the Towers for two or three weeks, when one Saturday afternoon she arrived home in a state of the greatest excitement, bearing a covered basket in her arms.

"Oh, Aunt Alice," she cried, as she met her Aunt at the door, "I have the loveliest, darlingest little black and white puppy, and he's all my own. Mr. Cardwell gave him to me. We were looking out of the window at his mother rolling him over and over, and there were three more, one yellow and brown, and the other all black and—"

"Stop, stop! Not quite so fast," said Aunt Alice. "I don't want to disappoint you, but we cannot keep dogs here, and you should not have brought him before asking leave first."

"But Mr. Cardwell gave him to me, he really did."

"Yes, very kind of him, but I can't let you have a dog. There are many reasons against it."

Aunt Alice walked down to the gate and asked the groom to wait. He had as usual brought Faith back in the dogcart.

Faith stood hugging her basket with scarlet cheeks and excited eyes. Charity and Hope besought her to open the basket. She did so.

"Oh, I must keep him!" she cried. "I must, I must. Aunt Alice wouldn't be so cruel! He's such a darling! He licked my face and fingers with his dear little pink tongue!"

The puppy looked at the three little faces anxiously bending over him, and gave a feeble squeak of approval. Aunt Alice came hurriedly into the Cottage and sat down at her desk to write a note. The children looking at her felt the puppy's fate was sealed, and Faith burst into a flood of tears.

"It's a shame!" she sobbed. "I've been planning all the way home about him, and where he will live. There's an old tub in the yard, and I will go without some of my breakfast and dinner so as to give him some!"

"Yes, we all will," said Charity eagerly. "I'm sure Granny would let us keep him. I'll run and ask her."

But Granny was out, and Aunt Alice was quite determined. Faith actually had a tiny struggle with her aunt before the basket could be taken out of her arms; but it was no good; the puppy was delivered back to the groom with the note for Mr. Cardwell, and Aunt Alice turned to confront three very miserable and rather sullen little nieces.

"Don't be foolish, unreasonable children!" she said. "And, Faith, stop crying at once. We are not well enough off to start keeping a dog in these war times. The licence would be expensive to begin with, and we want every crumb of food ourselves. I have to keep a cat because of the mice, and I can't have another animal to feed as well. It was very kind of Mr. Cardwell, but I have explained to him that we never have kept dogs, and cannot begin it now. Granny would be quite of the same opinion as myself. It was only the other day she refused the offer of a spaniel from Sir George."

Faith rushed away out into the orchard, sobbing her heart out. There was a thick hedge at the bottom of it, and here behind as old apple tree out of sight of the house she cried most bitterly. It was a grievous disappointment to her. She could not follow her Aunt's reasons, and thought she was cross and unkind to act so.

"Aunt Alice might understand—she doesn't care a bit, she's always being cross now. Oh, my darling puppy! It's cruel to take you away!"

As the tears fell fast, recollection came to her. Was there any need to go on crying so? Was not the Comforter close by?

"I don't want to stop crying!" she sobbed to herself. "I've a right to cry. Aunt Alice has made me cry, and she doesn't care a bit. She's horrid and unkind. No, I really don't want the Comforter at all. I want to cry."

And so with more anger than sorrow in her little heart, she sobbed on.

When supper time came, Charity came to hunt for her, and brought her indoors with a tear-stained face.

Aunt Alice took no notice of her unhappiness, but talked very cheerfully about taking them all out on an expedition in a few days' time.

"I have heard of a place where some wild strawberries grow, and we will take our dinner with us and bring home as many as we can carry. I have told Miss Vale that she must give you a whole holiday."

Charity and Hope clapped their hands; but Faith did not even smile. Her Granny spoke to her lovingly before she went to bed, but she made little response. Aunt Alice told her not to be sulky, and that made her feel worse. When she went upstairs to bed she felt she was the most ill-used little girl in all the world. But when she knelt down to say her prayers, better thoughts began to come to her.

"I did think I should never feel unhappy again because of the Comforter," she thought. "I suppose He has gone away quite disgusted with me, I don't feel Him near me now. I just feel angry still, because I'm so disappointed! And I don't care about the strawberries a bit. I wanted the puppy. But nobody cares. Even Charity and Hope, who seemed to want him, have quite forgotten all about him now, and they laugh and talk and think me silly not to laugh too. Oh, please, God, do send the Comforter back. Perhaps He would make me feel good again. I don't feel it now. I'm sorry for being so cross."

Faith was getting rather near comfort now. When once she had owned that she had been in the wrong she began to feel better.

And before she fell asleep that night she had the feeling that the Comforter was near her, and that she was being made happy once more.

When the next morning dawned she found that the sun was shining and the birds singing, and life before her was bright, as it always was.

And she was quite ready to talk enthusiastically over the strawberry gathering. Charity and Hope were accustomed to her moods. They knew she felt things more deeply than they did, and were thankful to see her scamper out into the orchard before breakfast, and come in singing under her breath, as she pulled her chair towards the table.

Nobody alluded to the trouble of yesterday, and, child-like, Faith soon pushed it into the background, and threw herself into the present without a shadow of care or disappointment upon her little face.

CHAPTER X
STRAWBERRY PICKING

THE strawberry gathering was a great success. It was a long walk, but when at last they reached the spot, and found a sloping and rather uncultivated piece of ground covered with red strawberries, the children screamed with delight. There was a stream at the bottom, and a wood on the upper side. Hope said with ecstasy:

"It has everything we want, Aunt Alice. We can get wood to light a fire, and water for the kettle to boil."

"Yes," said Aunt Alice, who seemed as happy as the children: "I only wish that dear Granny was here to enjoy it too, but it would have been too long a walk for her. I have a dream sometimes of getting a donkey and a little trap, then Granny could drive and enjoy the country as we do."

"Oh, Aunt Alice, how lovely! Do get a donkey," pleaded the children.

But Aunt Alice shook her head.

"How do you think we could afford to buy one? It's just as much as we can do to feed and clothe you all."

"It's a pity we aren't birds," said Faith; "then we could fly about and feed ourselves. Don't you think we might live on wild things? Strawberries and nuts and mushrooms—they don't cost money, do they?"

"We won't talk of money now," said Aunt Alice cheerfully, "let us all pick as hard as we can. If we get a great many baskets full, I may be able to make some jam."

So they set to work. The strawberries were very small, and it took a long time to fill a basket, but the little girls were perfectly happy. The novelty of it delighted them.

And then when dinner time came, Aunt Alice said they would all have an hour's rest. She sat down with a newspaper at the foot of a tree, but the children could not keep still. They dashed into the wood and brought out armfuls of sticks, and Aunt Alice gave them a match. It was some time before the fire would burn. They had not much experience in fire building out of doors, but at last they were successful, and then the little tin kettle, which Aunt Alice had brought in her basket, was taken down to the stream and filled with water, and placed on the fire.

Aunt Alice put down her newspaper, and unpacked her basket. The kettle soon boiled, and cups of tea, with bread and cheese sandwiches, hard-boiled eggs and plain slices of cake seemed a very nice and unusual dinner to the children.

"Oh," said Hope, "if only we could always have meals out of doors."

"Then one day," said Aunt Alice, "you would all come to me and say:

"'Please, for a very great treat may we have dinner indoors to-day? It would be so lovely to sit up on proper chairs and a real table, and have no buzzing flies or nasty caterpillars crawling over our food.'"

As she finished speaking, Aunt Alice fished a caterpillar out of her tea.

Charity looked thoughtful.

"Perhaps we should feel like that," she said; "it's because we never do it that we like to do it now."

"That's it," said her Aunt; "it's the unexpected and unusual that pleases us so."

"But if I was rich," said Charity, knitting her brows, "I could have something new every day. I should like to have a big house and a lot of visitors, and I would give them surprises every day."

"Well now, let's pretend you are rich," said Hope, "and Granny and Aunt Alice and Faith and I would come and see you. What surprises could you give us? Tell."

Charity sat up and hugged her knees. Her eyes were away on some distant hills. She was silent for a moment or two, then she began to speak.

"The first morning after breakfast I would lead Granny down the steps, and there would be waiting for her a beautiful little pony carriage painted blue with white velvet cushions, and two white Arab ponies with flowing manes and tails, and a little boy would get up on the seat behind and fold his arms and Granny would step in and take the reins in her hands and drive away miles into the most beautiful country she has ever seen. Granny likes driving herself. She always used to do that, when she was rich, didn't she, Aunt Alice?"

"I don't think dear Granny was ever rich," said Aunt Alice, laughing.

"Oh, go on, Charity! What about me?" asked Hope.

Charity smiled radiantly.

"Oh, of course, I would give you a horse to ride, and six dogs, and a part of the garden, which would be wired into a little zoo, and there would be all kinds of animals in it, and at the side a hospital where you would doctor the sick ones and mend their broken legs."

"Oh, how heavenly!"

"And Faith," went on Charity, "would have to come out with me, and pay visits to all kinds of wonderful old men with beards. Some would live in cottages, and give her baked apples for tea, some would live in beautiful houses, but they would all be very glad to see her and would sit up and talk with her for hours."

"Oh," cried Faith, clapping her hands, "I think I should have the best, for my surprise would be fresh every day. I could see one new old man every day, and Charity and Granny would soon come to the end of theirs. What about Aunt Alice?"

Charity looked thoughtful.

"I should take her one day into the drawing-room, and there would be a tall, nice, smiling man, with manners like a prince. And then I should shut the door and go away, and he would ask her to marry him, and he would take her away to a house nearly as big as mine—not quite, perhaps."

"You ridiculous child!" laughed Aunt Alice.

"Mrs. Cox always said you ought to get married," said Charity, "she said you were too young and pretty to be an old maid."

"Well," said Aunt Alice, "you would be quite a fairy godmother to us all, Charity, but, my dear child, the novelty of riches even wears off after a time. If you can have everything you want, you soon want nothing, and that stage brings discontent as well as content."

The children could not follow this.

They finished their lunch, washed their cups and plates up in the stream; then set to work picking strawberries again.

Later on they had an early tea before they started to walk home. And as they were in the middle of it who should come riding by but the Pirate. He recognised the children and rode up to them, dismounting, and talking to Aunt Alice for some minutes. Then she asked him if he would like a cup of tea, and he said he would love it. So he tied his horse to a tree stump, and sat down upon the ground with them. The little girls chattered to him freely; and he told them some very funny stories about people and animals he had met abroad. He stayed quite a long time; and agreed with the children that meals in the open air tasted much better than in the house.

"Give me a tent and a gun and a fishing rod," he said, "and I would want nothing else if sport were good."

"Have you ever had a tent?" asked Hope.

"Yes, I went a shooting expedition in Africa with two Kaffirs," he said; "but that journey ended disastrously for me. I had to swim a river and couldn't change my clothes, and had a bout of rheumatic fever which nearly finished me, and has left me a crock to the end of my days!"

A shadow came over his face. They all felt very sorry for him, and then he laughed but not very happily.

"So that's why I funk at home, instead of taking my place in the fighting line," he said.

"There's a lot of hard fighting being done at home," said Aunt Alice quietly.

He looked at her, and when their eyes met, they understood each other. The young man was not the only one who was doing his duty at home without getting any praise or honour for it. Aunt Alice was doing the same, and she knew that it was hard work sometimes.

He accompanied them home and let the little girls ride his horse in turn, he walking by their side and talking to Aunt Alice about many things.

"My Nora is as quiet and steady as a rock," he said; "so you need not be afraid she will run away from you."

"She likes to walk with you, doesn't she?" said observant Hope; "she keeps looking round to see if you are there!"

"Yes, Nora and I are fast friends. We've been twelve years together now."

He insisted upon carrying most of the baskets, and when they reached home Faith hastily whispered something into her Aunt's ear.

She smiled.

"Faith wants to send your father some of these strawberries to taste. What do you think about it?"

"He'll be awfully pleased, of course."

So Faith ran indoors and got a tiny pet basket of her own, and filled it with strawberries. She tied a red ribbon round it, and asked the young man to give it to his father with her "dearest love."

He promised to do so, and then the little girls ran indoors to tell Granny of their happy day.

Faith was much delighted the next day when a note arrived for her from old Mr. Cardwell. She opened it with much pride and showed it to everyone:

"DEAR LITTLE MISS MOTH,

"I thank you for your kind thought for a cross old man. The berries were really too pretty to be eaten. But to please you I have devoured them, and have been taken back to my boyhood's days. I know the spot where they grow. When you come next Saturday, I will tell you an anecdote concerning them.

"Your old friend,
"W. CARDWELL."

"He isn't a cross old man to me," said Faith. "I like him next to Timothy."

"I shouldn't like to be called Miss Moth," said Charity; "a moth is a horrid, dusty thing—lives on old clothes; the Bible says it corrupts, that's an awful thing to do."

Faith's face fell.

"I hope I don't corrupt," she said; "what does it mean?"

"Well, you do like old things," said Hope; "you like old men, so that part fits you."

"I think corrupt means make rotten or bad," said Charity.

"How dreadful!" said Faith. "I'm sure Mr. Cardwell didn't mean to call me anything horrid. I'll ask him. But I think he thought I looked like a moth, he said I came into his room like one."

"And you're easily crushed," said Charity laughing; "yes, you're rather like a moth in that way."

Then she said:

"Hope and I mean to get a special friend. Of course we have Sir George, but we mean to get somebody else. And I know who it will be!"

"Who is it?" asked Faith.

But Charity nodded her head mysteriously.

"Somebody I've met. You haven't met them. It's awfully nice in the country, we're always finding out new people."

She would say nothing more to Faith, but whispered in corners to Hope; and Faith did not like that at all.

Charity was a little bit jealous of Faith going off to the Towers every Saturday afternoon. Nothing stopped it. If it was a wet day, a closed carriage arrived for her.

And Hope said, laughing, one day when Charity, with a sulky face, watched Faith driving away, "We won't be like Cinderella's sisters, Charity. Faith is rather like Cinderella, isn't she? But we won't be cross about it."

And then it was that Charity began to think about finding some new friend to be quits with Faith.

She was marvellously successful.

One Saturday she and Hope were taking a walk across some fields to a farm; their Aunt had sent them to fetch some eggs. On the way they passed a lady sitting on a campstool making a sketch of an old ruined mill by the stream. She looked up and smiled at them as they passed her, and made some remark about the weather. The little girls were rather shy and went on to the farm. They discovered that the artist's name was Miss Huntingdon, and that she had come to the farm to lodge for the summer. Mrs. Davis, the farmer's wife, loved to talk, and she told the children all about her.

"I did use to be her nurse—Miss Mary was always my favourite— she had three brothers—and now she lives in a big house in London with her father—he have got war work and so did Miss Mary have—but she broke down, and the doctors said she must rest in the country, and so she have come down here. A beautiful painter she be! She always painted, Miss Mary did, and many's the time I punished her for daubing her white pinnies all over with paint."

The little girls listened to this and much more, and they had seen Miss Huntingdon several times since, and thought she had a very nice face. Charity now determined to make friends with her.

She and Hope set out one warm afternoon in July to track her down. They knew she painted by the river, and it was not long before they found her. But it needed some courage to go up and begin making acquaintance with her.

Hope's courage gave out: she hid behind a tree, whilst Charity crept boldly forwards, until she reached Miss Huntingdon, who was very busy making a pretty sketch of the river and the fields beyond.

"Oh," sighed Charity, "how I wish I could paint!"

Miss Huntingdon turned her head and smiled at her. "Do you? Have you ever tried?"

"We paint pictures for scrap-books," said Charity, waxing confidential; "but we haven't very good paints. Not like yours. May I watch you? And may Hope? She's afraid to come near."

"Oh, you mustn't be afraid of me," said Miss Huntingdon, laughing; "and I'm rather a sociable person. I like to have people to talk to. You see, I can paint and talk at the same time. I have seen you before, haven't I? Do you live near here?"

Charity beckoned to Hope, then began eagerly telling Miss Huntingdon all about themselves. Before long Hope was brave enough to put in her word, and Miss Huntingdon plainly showed them that she would like to be friendly. Charity told her that they knew Mrs. Davis and often got eggs from her.

"Next time you come over you must let me know you are there. I have such a dear old sitting-room at the Farm."

"May we be friends with you?" asked Charity eagerly.

Miss Huntingdon laughed aloud.

"You are the quaintest children I have ever seen!" she said.

Hope felt compelled to explain Charity's somewhat forward behaviour.

"It's really because Faith makes friends with old men, and we want to make friends with somebody else. Faith goes out to tea every Saturday to the Towers, and Charity and I have to stay at home."

"Oh, I see daylight. Faith is your other sister, is she not? And you would like to come to tea with me on Saturday? I shall be delighted. It will cheer me up. And I'll get Mrs. Davis to make one of her big tea-cakes. That's settled, then, and I shall expect you next Saturday at four o'clock."

Charity and Hope were very uncomfortable. Charity said:

"We never meant to ask you to ask us. And Granny and Aunt Alice mightn't let us come. It's very kind of you, but if you'll let us come and talk to you while you are painting sometimes and be friends, we would like to do that, without coming to tea."

Miss Huntingdon looked at Charity's red cheeks and Hope's downcast eyes and understood.

"Very well," she said; "we'll just be friends and tea will come later on. Now I've finished my sketch for to-day, so must say good-bye to you. And I shall be here every afternoon this week, so you will know where to find me."

Charity and Hope went home and informed Faith that they had got a charming friend and would be very often away in the woods with her.

Faith of course was curious, but for some time she could not find out who it was.

And then one day Granny and Aunt Alice went to tea with Lady Melville and met Miss Huntingdon, and Aunt Alice and she became the greatest friends. But Charity and Hope still maintained that they had the first claim upon her, and the invitation to take tea with her came and was accepted.

They went to the Farm when Faith went to the Towers and all seemed satisfied.

CHAPTER XI
THE GREY DONKEY

THE summer holidays came at last and Miss Vale said good-bye to her pupils for six weeks.

Charlie Evans had been away with his mother for a month at the seaside. Now he returned looking as brown as a berry and much stronger in every way. He came round to the Cottage the first evening after his return home, and the little girls took him into the orchard, where they had been trying to erect a kind of tent with an old piece of sacking and four stout sticks, which wobbled about in the ground at the least touch. Charlie did not think much of their attempt.

"Why don't you get a man to put the poles in?" he said. "I know a chap who would do it. The blacksmith's son. He comes once a week to do up our garden."

"But he would want to be paid," said Charity, anxiously.

"No, he wouldn't. He's very fond of me. I'll ask him as a favour. What's the tent going to be? A wigwam or a hunting box or a gipsy encampment?"

"Which do you think would be nicest?" asked Hope.

Charlie cocked his head on one side and considered.

"A hunting box—at least, a tent pitched near an African jungle. If you get it made tight and taut, I'll come round to-morrow morning with some of my hunting trophies, and I'll still be Captain, and my wife must make the tent comfortable and do the cooking, and Bolt and Ben must come out hunting with me. Will your aunt let me spend the day here, if I bring some food? You can't hunt unless you have the whole day out."

"Oh, we'll ask her," said Charity excitedly; "but you must get the tent fixed properly."

"All right," said Charlie, "I'll go and get the man, and you go in and tell your aunt about it."

He marched off up the village, and Granny and Aunt Alice were besought by the little girls for leave to spend a whole day out in the orchard without any interruption.

"And if you could give me something real to cook," said Charity, following her aunt into the kitchen, "something that I could put into a pot, and boil over a real fire."

Aunt Alice not only gave them leave to have Charlie for the whole day, but said she would give them what they wanted for dinner and tea.

"Only mind this," she said, "you must not be running backwards and forwards to the house all day long. Get what you want in the morning, and stay out all day, as if you were having a picnic miles off from home. I shall not expect you in till tea-time, and you must get your wood for the fire yourselves, not take any of mine from the wood-shed. And be sure to have your fire out of reach of the apple trees, or you will be burning them."

The children were delighted.

"It is nice to have Charlie back," said Hope; "he always thinks of such jolly things."

Charlie was as good as his word. John Lucas, the blacksmith's son, came along, and soon made the tent firm for the children. He brought a couple of extra poles and made a splendid framework for a tent. Charity got hold of some more old sacks, and the little girls worked hard all that day making their tent as comfortable as they could.

The next morning they could hardly eat any breakfast from excitement. Aunt Alice gave them a little kettle and an old saucepan, and a few cracked cups and saucers. Then she made up a basket of food, and delivered it into Charity's hands.

When they went out into the orchard at nine o'clock, they found Charlie had already arrived. He had trundled a small wheelbarrow down from his home, with a lot of his pet possessions. They spent nearly an hour in adorning their tent. He had an old leopard skin, which was placed on the ground. Some curious assegais and old bows and arrows he fastened up inside, and then he showed the little girls about a dozen skins of different small animals, which he had cured and mounted himself. There was a badger's skin, a stoat's, a grey rat's, and four or five mole skins. These he pinned up round the tent with great pride. Then over the entrance, he fastened up with string a dreadful-looking skull. It really belonged to an old sheep, but he said:

"This keeps away Indians and bushrangers. It shows I kill my enemies with the greatest ease."

Then underneath the skull, he put up a big printed paper. The letters were all painted in red ink.

"Here lives Captain Charles, the Great Hunter and Lion Killer. Trespassers will be shot without warning."

"What will you shoot them with?" asked Charity.

Charlie produced his fire-arms promptly. He had an air gun, a bow and arrow, and a toy pistol. The little girls were quite awed.

Then began a very delightful day. Charity was perfectly happy peeling and boiling some potatoes and onions, and putting a bit of bacon in her saucepan over a wood fire, just outside the hut. Charlie went across the fields with Hope and Faith, tracking all kinds of wild animals. The only thing that spoiled Faith's enjoyment was that he actually shot a rat with his air gun; and when he pursued it into a corner behind a haystack, he finished it with a stout stick. Faith fled from him shuddering, when he held it up to her by its tail.

"You little stupid! It's a—a skunk—an awful smelling animal which needs to be buried at once, but it is a very good kind of creature to kill."

"Oh, bury it quick!" cried Faith, "Don't let me see the poor thing— it's cruel to kill anything."

"But I'm a hunter," said Charlie. "Oh, what a shame it is I have only girls to play with!"

"I'm not like Faith," asserted Hope. "Don't mind her, she's always fussing over dead things. Aunt Alice lets Spicer catch the mice, and this is a rat. There's no difference."

Faith tried to hide her horror. She liked the stalking after game, but she was always glad when the rabbit fled away, and the bird flew off out of reach of Charlie's gun.

At seven o'clock that evening, Aunt Alice went out to call the little girls in. She found them all sitting on the ground inside the tent listening to one of Charlie's stories. The fire was blazing away merrily outside. They were very loth to leave their play. Aunt Alice made them put out the fire, and Charlie took a reluctant departure. He left all his skins with them.

"I'm going to drive with Dad to-morrow, but perhaps I can come round the next day," he said. And then he went off.

"Oh, Aunt Alice, we have enjoyed ourselves," Charity said. "And our dinner was delicious. And in the afternoon I joined the hunters and we went through the woods for miles, and we saw a squirrel and a weasel. Charlie knows such a lot about the woods, and he knows every bird by name."

"Well, he can come over another day. As long as you do not get into any mischief, I don't mind him being with you."

So this was the beginning of many delightful days, and the holidays slipped by so fast that the little girls were quite sorry to think that lessons would soon begin again.

One afternoon, Faith was making a frock for one of her dolls. It had been raining. She was in the schoolroom alone. Charity and Hope were helping their aunt to make jam in the kitchen. Suddenly the schoolroom door opened and Hope dashed in.

"Faith, quick, come! There's a boy at the gate wants to see you, and he has such a beautiful big grey donkey."

Faith ran out of the house down to the gate. Then her face lighted up in pleased recognition.

"Why, it's Dan," she cried, "the gipsy boy who spilled his milk! How is your mother, Dan?"

"Dead," he said, meeting Faith's gaze very bravely.

Faith was quite shocked.

"Folks never left us alone," the boy said sadly. "They hustled mother into Infirmary, and then us heard father were shot dead, and we sold the van, and mother she said to me:"

"'I'd like that little girl to have Topsy. Take her to her, and tell her I'm dyin' happy—and don't forget what she telled me.'"

"We sold our horse—but I've tramped close on twenty-five mile with Topsy—she'll only want a field to feed in. Father used her for a small cart, but us got rid of that when he went to war, and mother's just kept Topsy on; her couldn't bear parting with her. She follers like a dog."

"Oh, Dan, it's a wonderful present!" cried Faith, with shining eyes. "But I feel I ought to pay for Topsy, and we can't do that because we're so poor."

"Mother left her to you. She didn't want her sold. She wanted her to have a good home."

"Oh, wait a minute! I must tell Aunt Alice. It would be too glorious if she lets me have her."

Faith dashed back to the house, and Aunt Alice came out, and had a long talk with the boy. He was going to join his uncle, who kept another van, but who did not want the donkey. And after a long talk Aunt Alice said that Faith might keep Topsy.

She was taken into the orchard, where she began to munch the grass very contentedly, and Dan was invited into the cottage. Aunt Alice gave him a cup of cocoa and some bread and cheese in the kitchen, and thanked him very much for bringing the donkey to Faith.

As for the little girls, they could hardly contain their joy. They hung round Topsy watching her every movement, but when Dan took his leave, Faith walked to the gate with him and wished him good-bye very gravely.

"We'll take the greatest care of Topsy, and if you ever pass this way again, you'll come and see her, won't you? Are you always going to live in a gipsy van? How lovely!"

"I just can't live in a stuffy 'ouse," Dan said.

And then he marched away, and Faith ran back to the orchard, thinking herself the happiest little girl in the whole world.

There was great discussion that evening as to how they should use Topsy.

"I suppose a saddle is very, very expensive?" Faith asked her aunt. "Of course, we could ride on a sack, couldn't we?"

"Yes, I'm afraid we can't afford a saddle at present," said Aunt Alice cheerfully. "I don't know that a cheap little cart wouldn't be better for you all. Then Granny could drive in it."

"Oh, that would be like Charity's story coming true," said Faith, with great delight.

"Let us all save up our money," suggested Charity.

But Hope and Faith said dolefully, "It would take years and years before we could get enough."

They had to be content with riding Topsy bare-backed. Hope thought nothing of jumping on her back and having a gallop. Faith and Charity went more gently with her—and then one day something wonderful happened.

It was Granny's birthday. The little girls had for some weeks been busily making their presents for her. Granny told them she always valued anything that they made her much more than what they bought for her.

So Charity had been making a big box pincushion out of an old soapbox. Hope had knitted her a warm pair of cuffs, and Faith had made her a bag to keep her knitting in, and had worked in big letters across it "Granny." These were put on the breakfast table in the morning, and Aunt Alice, who had bought a book, put her present with them.

Granny was always a delightful receiver of gifts. She looked so astonished, and delighted, and was so full of praise and thanks, that her grandchildren had the feeling that their presents were really wonderful, and "just the things Granny was wanting!"

They were all talking and kissing and laughing, when there came a sharp knock at the door. Aunt Alice went to open it, and found there the groom from the Hall with a note from Sir George. Whilst Granny was reading it, the little girls happened to look-out of the window, and there they saw outside the gate a delightful little basket carriage with brown cushions and brown wheels. In their excitement, they flew out of the cottage to inspect it, and in a minute, Granny came down to the gate with tears in her eyes.

"It's too much!" she murmured. "Too good altogether!"

And then the children were told that it was a birthday present for Granny from Sir George and Lady Melville. And in the little carriage was packed a complete set of brown harness. Granny let the children see her birthday letter:

"MY DEAR OLD FRIEND,

"My wife and I join in giving you loving and heartfelt wishes for your birthday. I have not forgotten the date, and as I have heard of the addition of a donkey to your household, I venture to hope that this little basket tub may be useful to you all. If I see you driving about our lanes, it will remind me of old times, and I know that your unselfish heart will rejoice that your birthday gift can be shared by your little family. May you be spared to us for many years. Mary sends her best love.

"One of your old boys,
"GEORGE MELVILLE."

The excitement was intense now. Aunt Alice felt glad that they had a stable in which they could house the little carriage. Of course that same afternoon Topsy was harnessed, and the children and Granny had a triumphal drive through the village, Aunt Alice walking after them. Topsy did not go very fast—but nobody wished her to do so at present. It was quite enough joy to the children to sit in state and watch Granny drive.

Faith was perhaps the most happy of all, for was it not her donkey that was the cause of Granny's wonderful birthday present?

Before many days had passed, all the little girls had learnt to drive, and Topsy was so reliable and steady that they could be trusted to drive about the lanes alone. Charity came in after her first time as driver in a great state of excitement:

"I really must write to Mrs. Cox," she said. "I have been meaning to do it for ever so long. I must tell her what a splendid time we are having. She always insisted we should be miserable in the country and be wishing ourselves back in London."

So she got out her little desk, and wrote the following letter—Hope and Faith both helped her with it. They had a great desire to impress Mrs. Cox with their prosperity—

"MY DEAR MRS. COX,

"I told you I would write and tell you how we got on in the country. We find it a very perfect place. We have a house, and a stable, and a field, all to ourselves. There is no next door on either side. We have apples all over our field, and grass as long as we like to let it grow. We have made a great many new friends who ask us to tea, and play games with us. One of Faith's friends gave her a beautiful present of a donkey. She is grey, and she loves bits of bread. We all ride her when we want to. One of Granny's friends gave her a carriage on her birthday, so we drive for miles whenever we have time. We have a governess and lessons, but it is holidays now.

"We have a tent in our field, and we have a boy friend who comes nearly every day to shoot and to fish with us. We have all kinds of wild animals near us. Rabbits and owls and squirrels and weasels. And there are hundreds of birds who all sing at once early in the morning. We have fields where little strawberries grow wild, and we can pick them without paying anything. And we never go out for a walk without seeing somebody we know. We have all kinds of friends, a lady who paints pictures, a shepherd who keeps a dog to drive his sheep, a boy who has a raft of his own, a man who plays he is a pirate, an old man who lies on a couch, and is very fond of Faith, a man who has a house full of books, and his wife who always smiles when she sees us, and they both have horses and ponies which Hope likes to ride. And they have two boys who are very nice, but we like Charlie best.

"And now, Mrs. Cox, you see how happy we are in the country, and we hope you are well, and if you would ever be able to come and see us we will be very glad to take you round and show you everything.

"From your affectionate friends,
"CHARITY, HOPE and FAITH."

"It doesn't sound as if we are bragging?" said Hope a little doubtfully after Charity had read this long letter through with much pride.

"No, for we only tell her what is true," Charity replied.

"I should like you to tell her a little more about Timothy," said Faith. "Mrs. Cox would be made quite happy if Timothy talked to her."

"Mrs. Cox would never be happy," said Charity firmly; "she's one of those people who are happy when they're unhappy."

"Let me put a postscript," begged Faith.

Charity assented, and Faith sat down at the table and wrote very carefully as follows:

"My friend Timothy tells me about God the Comforter Who lives now in the world going about and drying people's tears. Do you know Him, Mrs. Cox? He will make the people you tell us about who are sick of life quite, quite joyful. I wish you knew Timothy. He does talk me into being happy, and you would be happy too. But the Comforter is in London and in your street. I told Timothy where you lived and he said He was.

"FAITH."

Charity and Hope looked at each other when they had read what Faith had written.

Charity shrugged her shoulders.

"Faith will get too good to live soon," she said; "but she's simply cracked over her old Timothy."

Faith coloured up, but said nothing. She could never argue, and found it wisest to be silent.

But she was not sorry that she had sent Mrs. Cox that postscript.

CHAPTER XII
THE ACCIDENT

THE Hall was closed for two months. Sir George and Lady Melville had taken their boys to Scotland, so the little girls were shut up entirely to Charlie for society. They quarrelled with him occasionally. Once he went off and stayed away from them for a whole week. But he found he missed them quite as much as they missed him, and on the whole they were very good friends.

One afternoon they were all playing in the orchard when they saw the Pirate ride up to the cottage, tie up his horse and go inside.

He very often called now; sometimes he brought Granny fruit; sometimes he said he came to ask Aunt Alice's advice on some knotty point. He did not always ask to see the little girls, so they went on with their games. Presently Faith was called. She ran in and was met by her aunt with a very grave face.

"Faith, Mr. Cardwell wants you to go back with him. His father is taken very ill and wants to see you."

Faith looked almost frightened:

"Oh, how dreadful, Aunt Alice! Does he want me to nurse him?"

Her aunt smiled.

"No, child, he has a nurse already. Run upstairs and put on your hat and jacket. And be quick! Don't keep Mr. Cardwell waiting."

The young man was standing on the doorstep; he looked at Aunt Alice pleadingly:

"Won't you come?"

She shook her head.

"He does not know me, and if he is conscious, he would not like to see strangers. Take care of Faith and remember she's a highly-strung child, and if she can't do him any good, don't let her stay in his room. Don't give up hope. He may pull round. I am so sorry for you."

They shook hands, and Faith, running downstairs, was lifted up in front of Mr. Cardwell's horse, and he rode away with her.

"Just like a pirate or a bandit," said Hope, looking over the hedge.

They thought she had been taken off to have tea with the old man, but they were soon told the truth.

Faith was taken upstairs when she got to the Towers, and the big bedroom into which she was shown quite awed her. A nurse in uniform came forward at once. She looked surprised when she saw Faith.

"Is it this tiny child he wishes to see?" she said, looking at the young man doubtfully.

He nodded.

"I think it is. We'll see."

And then Faith was led up to the big bed, and was lifted up to sit on the edge of it.

Old Mr. Cardwell looked to her, as if he were asleep. Only his lips moved—and he muttered below his breath.

"Speak to him, Faith. Don't be afraid. He's so fond of you," whispered the Pirate.

So Faith put her soft little hand on that of the invalid's.

"It's little Miss Moth, please. I've come to see you."

The old man opened his eyes drowsily. Quite a smile hovered about his lips.

"Little—Miss Moth—come—to say good-bye—" he murmured; "so glad."

The nurse moved away, and so did the young man.

Then she took up his hand and kissed it.

"Don't go just yet, unless God wants you very much."

He shook his head quickly.

"Say—say—something—to go with me."

Faith looked puzzled. Then her face brightened.

"You mean you want somebody to go up to Heaven with you?"

He looked at her steadily and earnestly—tried to speak and could not.

"The Comforter will go with you, I'm sure," said Faith, cheerfully. "Timothy says He never leaves people till He puts them into God's arms. He'll show you the way. Oh, I wish I could come too!"

Her eyes were shining as she spoke.

"Is that what you mean? Is it the Comforter you want?"

But old Mr. Cardwell lay still, and there was a smile on his lips. The troubled look had left his face, his head fell back on the pillows. The nurse came quickly up, and she and Faith caught one murmured word from the old man's lips. It was "Jesus."

Then Faith was taken out of the room rather quickly. She waited downstairs perplexed and troubled, wondering if her old friend were really going to die, wondering what he had wanted her to say, and wishing she could go back to the bedroom again.

Presently the Pirate came down to her.

There was a strange look on his face; Faith thought there were almost tears in his eyes.

"Do you remember my telling you what a good thing it would be if my father could believe in the Comforter Whom you talked to me about one day when we were on the bridge together?"

"That was before I knew you very well," said Faith, putting her mind back to the occasion mentioned. "You said I could come and see him and talk to him. And then I did."

"Yes, you did, and I really believe, little Faith, that my father was made a happy old man at last. He has been so different lately, and he was calling for you this afternoon."

"Is he really going to heaven?" Faith asked.

"I hope he is there already," was the grave reply.

And then Faith understood that her old friend was dead. She was driven home by the groom, and she cried a little; and when she reached Granny went straight into her arms and finished her cry with her head against her shoulders.

"I didn't want him to die. He is one of my friends," she sobbed. "And I can't bear to think I shall never see him again."

"One day you will," said Granny, "and none of us must wish him here again. He suffered very much, and never could bear being ill. Now he has got beyond pain and will be comforted."

"But," said Faith quickly, "he could have been comforted here— everybody can, can't they, if they know about the Comforter?"

"Yes, yes," murmured Granny. She soothed Faith and talked softly to her about the happy entry into the Golden City of everyone who trusted in Jesus.

"Mr. Cardwell spoke to Jesus. He said His Name," said Faith. "I thought he wanted the Comforter."

"When we come to die," said Granny gravely, "it is our Saviour we want; for it was through His Death that we can go into Heaven. It is for His sake that we are forgiven and taken there."

Faith nodded.

"But the Comforter carries people up to Heaven. Timothy says he does."

And Granny said no more.

Faith missed her old friend very much in the days that followed. Charity and Hope often went over to the Farm to see Miss Huntingdon, but one day she was invited to go with them, and after that she did not feel so lonely. She still went up to Timothy's cottage and had long talks with him. Aunt Alice said to Granny that Faith was too old for her age.

"It isn't natural for a child to be talking to an old man continually."

"I don't know about that," said Granny smiling; "we old folk often understand children better than you younger ones. And Faith is a child at heart. She is just as keen in her games as the others, and I'm thankful to see her white cheeks becoming rosy. She is much stronger than she was. It is quite natural for a child to be religious, Alice."

"Is it? I suppose so. But even I should find Timothy very dull."

Aunt Alice had been up to Timothy's cottage once, and she had not enjoyed herself as much as Faith did. But that may have been because Timothy was very silent with her. He always brightened up when he talked to children.

The summer holidays came to an end; Miss Vale returned to her pupils, and lessons began again. Miss Huntingdon left the farm and went back to London. Both Charity and Hope were very sorry when she went, and missed going over to the farm to see her.

One day the Pirate came to wish the children good-bye.

He said he was going to shut up the Towers for a time, and go over to France.

It was Aunt Alice who received this confidence.

He and she were great friends, and he often asked her in the meekest voice what she would advise him to do.

Charity asked him if he were going to fight.

"No such luck!" he said. "But I've got a billet somewhere at the base. A friend of mine is out there, and he has pulled the necessary strings for me. I have nobody now who wants me in England."

"Oh, but we want you!" the children cried. "Do come back soon. Come back for Christmas."

"If the war is over, I will," he said cheerfully; then he took Faith aside:

"Will you sometimes go and see that my father's grave is kept tidy, Faith?"

"Oh," she said, with bright eyes, "I should love to do it. And may I plant some flowers on it? I have a garden of my own, and I should be so happy if you would let me."

"I shall be happy, too, if you will."

Then he put his hand on her curly head.

"God bless you, little Faith. I never can forget how you eased his last days!"

Then with a change of tone he added:

"And take care of your Aunt Alice; don't wear her out between you. If I come back and find her getting wrinkled, I shall carry her off away from you all!"

Faith laughed gaily.

"You really are a pirate," she said, "for you love carrying people away!"

"I mean it," he said, with a nod of his head.

It seemed quite dull when he went, for since his father's death he had come over very often to the Cottage.

Charlie was very sorry to lose him.

"I was getting to know him," he said; "he came over and brought me a fishing rod. He said crocks like me and him could be good fishermen if we were nothing else. And I mean to learn to be the best fisherman in the county."

Charlie always had a great idea of his own powers. He was still the Captain of his little company, and every spare afternoon would come to the tent in the orchard. One day he arrived with a new acquisition, a real telescope that he had found in an empty attic. It proved very useful in their games, and he soon found an opportunity to order Ben and Bolt up a tree to make observations of the country round.

"You must get up as high as you can, and if you see any of the enemy, however far off they may be, you must signal down to me without speaking where they are."

Hope and Faith were only too willing to climb any tree. They had sampled all the apple trees, but there was an oak tree at the bottom of the orchard which was much higher than any of the others, and they determined to climb up this. Hope carried the telescope. She was to spy through it, and Faith was to do the signalling by means of some toy flags. Charlie had taught them all to signal. There was not much about signalling that he did not know. Up the little girls went, higher and higher. They rather vied with each other as to who should get up the higher. Charity and Charlie were watching them from below, and egging them on.

"I don't think they had better climb any higher," said Charity a little anxiously; "the branches seem so thin."

"Oh, they're all right," Charlie cried. "Well, my men, what do you see?"

Hope was looking through the telescope now; she turned and said something to Faith, who was on a branch just below her.

Faith unrolled her flags. One of them slipped from her grasp. She made a hasty movement to catch it, and lost her balance. There was an awful crash of branches, a scream, and a heavy thud, and poor little Faith lay a huddled-up heap at the foot of the tree!

Charity rushed to pick her up, and rent the air with her screams:

"She's dead! Faith is dead! Aunt Alice! Granny! Come quick! Faith is killed."

Granny and Aunt Alice heard the cries and ran out. Aunt Alice picked up the unconscious child and carried her into the house, and up to her bed. Charlie's father was sent for, and happily he had just arrived home from his rounds, so no time was lost, but he looked very grave when he saw the little girl.

"It's extraordinary that no bones are broken," he said; "but she pitched on her head. It is concussion of the brain."

Faith was unconscious, but she was alive. The sobbing, frightened children in the orchard soon heard that bit of welcome news. Charlie was taken home by his father; Charity and Hope stole about the house on tiptoe. It had to be kept very quiet for many days, and Faith lay between life and death. Aunt Alice never left her. It was astonishing now that Faith was ill to find out how many friends she had in the village. All day long people were coming to enquire after the poor "little lady."

Old Timothy called in every evening on his way home from the farm.

Charity met him the first day with tear-stained eyes.

"Isn't it the most awful thing to happen!" she said. "And Mrs. Horn says that perhaps Faith will never get well in her head again. She says children have been turned into idiots for less than what Faith did. Oh, do ask God to make her quite well again! She's so fond of you. She doesn't know anybody now, but she called out this morning, 'I want the Comforter.' You told her all about Him, didn't you?"

Old Timothy nodded his head sadly.

"Bless her little heart, she learns me as much as I learn her. Her name is just right. She's just faith through and through! I only wish mine were as big. But there! Don't you fret, Missy; she's in the Lord's Hands, and whether He carries her Home or leaves her with us, 'tis all for the best."

"But it isn't for the best if Faith dies!" cried Charity, stamping her foot. "We don't want her to die. You don't care for her like we do, and Hope and I think it's all your fault. You made her so good that now she's got to die. All good children do!"

And then Charity burst into tears and ran back into the Cottage.

She and Hope could do no lessons for the first few days; and then as Faith still remained unconscious day after day they begged for Miss Vale to come to them again.

"We can't play, and the days are so long, and there's nothing to do," they wailed.

It was a relief to have their minds employed by sums and history and geography. Miss Vale was very kind, and had them over one day to tea with her. At another time they would have enjoyed themselves tremendously, for Miss Vale and her mother lived in an old-fashioned house in the High Street of the market town, and there was a lot to be seen from the window, and old Mrs. Vale was a bright, talkative old lady with such a lot of anecdotes which she delighted in telling them, that Charity and Hope were quite fascinated. But their thoughts never wandered very far from Faith on her sick bed.

"It seems so wonderful," said Charity to Miss Vale one day, "that just in one moment such awful things can happen. Faith was climbing and talking and laughing, and then the very next minute she was almost dead, and she's never spoken to us since!"

"And perhaps she'll never speak to us again," said Hope dismally; "and I had just been cross to her. She said she was a little afraid, and I called her a baby!"

Miss Vale comforted them as best she could.

When they had finished their lessons, they hardly knew what to do with themselves. They felt it was heartless to play in the orchard. Charlie was not allowed to come round to them. His father was very angry with the part he had played in the catastrophe.

One afternoon, Charity and Hope went up to the village shop. Mrs. Budd, who kept it, asked anxiously about Faith.

"I can't forget 'er a-turning to my old mother who was cryin' somethin' fearful one day in the shop. We'd just had a wire to say our John was killed out in France. The little dear took hold of her hands and stroked them, and began telling her how to be comforted, and she told her to go to see Timothy Bendall, and he would tell her how she would be made happy. And Mother did, she went up the very nex' day. She were fair distracted with grief, and couldn't keep still in her house. The old man did her a world of good, and he often drops in to have a chat with her. But 'twas Miss Faith who started to talk to her. Dear soul! To think she be lyin' there dyin'!"

"Oh, we hope she's going to get better," said Charity, with a troubled face. "Dr. Evans says we must hope."

They came out of the shop feeling very depressed, and then they met Lady Melville coming out of the village almshouses. She stopped at once to speak to them.

"Oh, it's awful!" said Charity. "Faith doesn't know anybody yet. Do you think she ever will again? I went in to see her this morning, and she keeps moving her head from side to side and moaning, and her hair is all cut quite short. It doesn't seem as if it can be Faith lying there!"

"You poor dear children!" said kind Lady Melville. "I wonder if you would both like to come and stay at the Hall till Faith's better. Do you think Granny would let you? It need not stop your lessons, for Miss Vale might come up to us and give them to you in the boys' old schoolroom. Shall I come and ask Granny about it?"

Charity and Hope looked quite delighted.

"Oh, it would be lovely!" Charity said. "Aunt Alice is always telling us to 'hush,' and we have to creep about all day on tiptoe. We don't want to hurt poor Faith, but it is so difficult to remember all day long!"

Lady Melville went straight back to the Cottage with them, and had a long talk with Granny and Aunt Alice.

An hour later Granny was driving the little girls with their small luggage up to the Hall.

Charity stroked Topsy's nose when they got out of the carriage.

"Do you think he knows Faith is ill, Granny? He seems rather melancholy to-day."

"I expect he misses your games with him in the orchard," said Granny.

"We don't like the orchard now," said Hope; "and I've quite made up my mind that I'll never climb again. Oh, Granny, is Faith going to get better?"

"If Faith gets through this week, Dr. Evans says she will recover," Granny said gravely.

She said good-bye to her little grand-daughters and drove away. They went into the house with sober faces.

But soon the novelty of their surroundings cheered them up. They had a large, cheerful bedroom with a soft, thick carpet and a cushioned couch and round table. Hope said it looked more like a sitting-room than a bedroom, and accustomed to the very plainest and barest of bedroom furniture, the little girls felt that they were in the lap of luxury.

And then they went into Lady Melville's morning room, where she and they had tea together.

Their tongues went fast. Lady Melville was a good listener, and they always felt thoroughly at home with her. When Sir George came in, two very cheerful children greeted him, and for the time Faith's illness was pushed into the background.

CHAPTER XIII
A WONDERFUL LEGACY

FAITH did get better, very slowly. And it was a happy day for Charity and Hope when they were able to go over from the Hall and see her sitting up and taking notice of everybody once again. She looked very small and white, and spoke languidly, as if it were too much trouble to get her words out, but she listened to her sisters' account of their days at the Hall with much interest.

"I ride on a pony every afternoon," said Hope with pride. "Tommy is much faster than Topsy. I go for rides with Sir George, and yesterday we rode into town, and I saw Mrs. Vale sitting in her window, and she nodded to me!"

"And I drove out with Lady Melville," said Charity, "and we went to tea with some friends of hers, and they said the war would soon be over, perhaps by Christmas."

Faith smiled, but made no comment on these bits of news; then she asked:

"Have you seen Timothy?"

"Not lately," answered Charity.

"I should like to see him," said Faith slowly.

Aunt Alice was in the room and heard her wish.

"Then you shall see him, darling. Charity, you can call at his cottage on your way home. Ask him to come the first day he can."

So Charity and Hope called at the little cottage.

The woods were just now in their autumn colours. Blackberries were fast getting ripe, and nuts lay ready on the ground to pick up. They lingered by the way to enjoy it all, and then they found Timothy outside, getting an armful of firewood. Sandy bounded forward to meet them.

When Hope patted his head and spoke to him, he whined a little and moved away.

"He's disappointed 'tisn't Miss Faith," said Timothy; "how is the little dear?"

"She wants to see you," said Charity; "will you go and see her as soon as you can? Aunt Alice told us to ask you."

"Ay, surely I will. Bless her little heart, there's not a day but I wonders how she is. I've missed her sorely. And I'm not the only one."

"No," said Hope with an understanding nod; "it is everybody that misses Faith. We wonder why, because we thought her rather quiet and dull sometimes, but we don't now. We know how we miss her, but we don't quite understand why the village people talk about her so."

"'Tis just her little winning way and her big heart," said Timothy; "and then when she talks to folk, she has always something big to talk about."

"How do you mean?" asked Charity.

Old Timothy rubbed his head slowly. It was a way he had when he was thinking.

"I was reading in the Book t'other day," he said, "and it made me think how the little maid be as good as her name. Do you remember the gran' chapter of the heroes who lived by faith? 'Tis said amongst the list of their noble doin's, that 'through faith they obtained promises,' and 'out of weakness were made strong.' Now, through Miss Faith talkin' I know more than one body hereabout who have obtained most precious promises and have been made strong!"

Charity and Hope were silent. They wished the old man good-bye and went on to the Hall.

"I don't understand Timothy," said Hope at last, "he talks as if Faith preaches to people."

"No, she just talks," said Charity, "but I suppose she talks about the Things we don't talk about, and it does people good."

Hope said nothing more, but the little girls found themselves repeating to Lady Melville what the old man had said.

"Children are rather prigs when they talk goody," said Charity—"at least, we think they are; but Timothy seemed to say that Faith had been doing great things just like the Bible people."

"I don't think little Faith is at all a prig," said Lady Melville gently; "you know if we are very full of anything we can't help talking about it. It bubbles up at once like a little spring in the ground which gets over full when a storm of rain comes. Faith has a great realisation of the Holy Spirit, the Comforter, and because she believes He makes every sad person happy, she talks to everybody who is sad, about Him. She can't help doing it. Dear little Faith! Why, even when she talks to me, I feel myself stronger in my faith when she goes away!"

The little girls were silent for a moment. Then Charity said:

"I suppose she practises her name. Granny often tells us we ought to make our names good. When I grow up and get rich, I shall give a lot of money away in charity; then I shall be acting out my name, shan't I?"

Lady Melville smiled.

"It is rather strange, but in the chapter in the Bible which tells about your name it says that you can give all your goods to feed the poor, and yet have no charity. You may do it to get praise from God, or from men, and not because you love them. We have false ideas of charity. It means love. You can love God, and everybody, if you are quite poor, and so be acting out your name now."

Charity thought over this.

"It says Charity is better than Hope or Faith," said Hope; "I wonder why. Charity often reminds me and Faith of that."

Charity hung her head.

"Well," said Lady Melville cheerfully, "I often tell you that you have all three beautiful names which ought to inspire you. Faith acts out hers without knowing it. If I were Charity, I should always try to be kind and loving to all, and not to think about myself at all, only of pleasing others. And if I were Hope, I should try to fill my mind with all the beautiful things we are told to hope for."

"I think my name is most difficult of all," said Hope, "because everything you hope for is always on in front of you; you never seem to catch it up!"

"Well," said Lady Melville smiling, "if we have got a sure hope of everything beautiful and happy coming to us in the future, we shan't mind about present troubles, and we shall be very happy people. You told me the other day that when Dr. Evans said there was hope of Faith's getting well again, you were so happy that nothing else seemed to matter. That is how we should all live. Nothing matters very much in this world because we have such beautiful, wonderful hopes about the next."

The little girls said no more, but they remembered Lady Melville's talk about their names, and it did them good.

They were very happy at the Hall, and very soon the day came when Granny said she could have them back at the cottage again. Faith was an invalid still. She seemed to be a long time in getting back her health and strength, but she was able to play with her dolls again, and go out for little walks; and she was bright and cheerful, and able now to talk nearly as fast as Charity and Hope.

Her birthday was the beginning of November. The children had a holiday. Charity and Hope went into town to buy her a birthday present. Their Aunt Alice was with them, and they had quite an exciting afternoon, for Aunt Alice took them to tea at the pastry-cook's, and the shops were very gay with preparations for Christmas. To add to their joy, they met Charlie and his mother, and Charlie was full of business. He had come into town to buy Faith a birthday present, and he took Charity and Hope off to a toyshop, whilst Mrs. Evans and Aunt Alice went into uninteresting shops, such as the grocer's and the linen-draper's.

"You see, I must get her something nice, because I made her ill," said Charlie; "at least, that is what father and mother say, but of course I didn't mean to. And what do you think I am going to buy her?"

The little girls could not guess.

"A box of fretwork tools. I had one once on my birthday, but my tools are broken and lost. It will be just the thing for Faith, for she can make things indoors, and I will come over and help her."

"That will be lovely," said Charity enthusiastically, "Hope and I are going to put our money together to make it more. We haven't very much only two shillings and fourpence."

They roamed round the toyshop. First they thought of a watering-can, but then they remembered that winter was coming and the flowers were over, so that Faith would not be able to use it for a long time. Then Hope suggested a paint box, but Faith was not so fond of painting as Charity was, so that was given up.

At last they saw a very cheap set of doll's tea things for half-a-crown. Aunt Alice, good-naturedly, had told them she would make their money up to 2s. 6d., so they got it.

"The cups will be quite big enough for us to drink out of," said Hope; "we can use them when we have feasts."

So the tea-set was bought. Granny's present for Faith was a little blue-knitted jacket to keep her warm when she went out. Granny had made it all herself. And Aunt Alice had bought her a little brown muff. There was great excitement when they got home that evening. Faith went to bed very early now; and after she was out of the way, the presents were all wrapped up in paper, and little tickets attached with the names of donors.

Somehow this birthday of Faith's seemed to be an extra important day. They could not help remembering how very nearly they had lost her.

And then Aunt Alice told Charity and Hope a secret, which was that old Mr. Cardwell had left a present for Faith which he had told his son to give her on her next birthday. The "Pirate" had left this with Aunt Alice before he went away, and Aunt Alice produced it now. It looked like a box, but Aunt Alice said she believed it was the old man's cabinet of coins which he had once showed to Faith. It was all carefully wrapped up in brown paper.

The next morning Charity and Hope were up early. Faith still had her breakfast in bed, but they were allowed to take their presents in before. As Faith sat up in bed unwrapping all her parcels, her little fingers trembled with excitement. There were cries of ecstasy over every one of the gifts. Faith was always easy to please. The tea-set was what she had always longed for, Granny's jacket was almost too grand to wear, and the muff was a luxury she had never before experienced. Charlie's box of fretwork was most entrancing; she longed to begin testing the tools at once; and then old Mr. Cardwell's present was slowly opened, with flushed cheeks, and shining eyes.

"Oh! Oh! It's his beautiful cabinet with all the old, old money in it! Look at the tiny drawers, and all the coins in different parts!"

Faith clasped her hands and almost cried.

"It seems as if he is alive," she said. "Oh! I wish he was! I wish he was!"

Charity and Hope were both as interested as she was in peeping into all the little drawers, and seeing all the varieties of ancient coin. Then in the bottom drawer Faith found a sealed envelope with her name written upon it. She looked at it with awe, for it was addressed by old Mr. Cardwell himself.

And then the next moment Aunt Alice was summoned to the room by the excited screams of the children.

"Granny! Aunt Alice! Quick! Faith has got one hundred pounds!"

It was true. The cheque in Faith's shaking hands was for one hundred pounds to be paid to Miss Faith Blair, and the little note was as follows:

"MY DEAR LITTLE MISS MOTH,

"I shall be gone away from you when you receive this, for I do not mean you to have it till after my death; and you will not get it until your birthday. It is in remembrance of a grateful old man, and, knowing your careful little soul, I want you to spend this money whilst you are young, in the best way that you can. Don't hoard it. Spend it on yourself and on others. There are no conditions attached to it. I humbly hope that you and I may one day meet each other again in that Land where you tell me everyone is welcome.

"Your old friend,
"W. CARDWELL."

Aunt Alice seemed stricken dumb, but she read the letter through, and passed it to Granny, who began to wipe her spectacles when she had finished it.

"Is it true?" asked Faith. "Can it be true that I've got a hundred pounds?"

"Yes, dear, it is. I'm sure I had no idea that such a present was in store for you."

Then Aunt Alice began to fold up the pieces of stray paper scattered over the bed.

"We must talk about it after breakfast," she said; "come along, children."

Charity and Hope went to their breakfast; but their talk was full of this wonderful gift.

"Why," said Charity, "Faith could buy a cottage of her own, couldn't she, with a hundred pounds?"

Aunt Alice laughed.

"Oh, no," cried Hope; "she wouldn't want anything uninteresting like that. She could buy a pony, and a saddle, and build a beautiful little stable for him all her own."

Granny began to smile now.

"We know that Charity would like a cottage, and Hope a pony, but what about Faith herself?"

"Oh, Faith never wants much," said Charity, "she's so easily pleased."

"And that is why old Mr. Cardwell could trust her with such a lot of money," said Aunt Alice, "he knew she wouldn't want to buy useless luxuries."

After breakfast, Faith was dressed, and brought downstairs. There was a bright fire in the cheerful living room where they generally sat, and before very long, Charlie arrived to give his best wishes for Faith's birthday, and to examine with her the contents of the fretwork box. He was much impressed when he heard the news.

"Why, you could buy a motor," he said; "that's what I should do."

But Faith's ambition did not lie in that direction.

"We have Topsy, and Granny's carriage, that's much nicer than a motor," she said.

"Well, what are you going to do with it?" he asked.

Faith looked dreamily into the fire. She was sitting in the old armchair, and a round table was pushed up to her side.

"I haven't got to settle to-day," she said. "I don't want to spend it all on one thing, I want to get lots of things."

"Make out a list, Faith," urged Charity. "Do it now."

But Faith would not be hurried. And Charlie was so anxious to start her cutting out patterns on wood with her fretwork saw, that she soon gave her whole attention to that. Charlie went home after lunch, but he was invited to come to tea, for there was a birthday cake, and Faith was going to pour out tea. Outside, it was wet and stormy, but the children were perfectly happy indoors that day, and Charity and Hope wrote down long lists of things that they would like Faith to buy with her money.

She was very tired when the exciting birthday was over; and when she was being tucked up into bed by her aunt, she said a little sadly:

"How can I thank Mr. Cardwell, Aunt Alice? It seems so dreadful not to take any notice, and not to thank him."

"It is what people call a legacy, dear. Only it was left to you in such a strange way. Nobody can thank for legacies, as they are left to them after the giver dies."

Faith lay still for a moment, then she said softly:

"Do you think that I might pray to God and ask Him if He would thank him for me. Would it be reverent to ask God to do that?"

"Yes, dear, I think you could pray about it."

So Faith waited till her aunt had left the room, and then she folded her hands and prayed in a whisper:

"Please, God, will you be so kind as to thank Mr. Cardwell for me, and will you tell him what a happy birthday I have had, and what an astonishing surprise it was to get that cabinet, and how I can hardly believe I have a hundred pounds all my own. I do thank him very, very much, and I thank you for letting me have it. Amen."

Downstairs Aunt Alice was saying to Granny:

"I hope it won't turn the child's head. Of course, it is much too big a sum to be handled by her. What should you advise, mother?"

"We must persuade her to put it into the bank for the present, and only draw a little at a time. He was a strange old man."

"Fred had no idea that it was anything beyond a cabinet. I must write to him about it, for of course this cheque can't be honoured."

Granny looked grave.

"I suppose not. The child may have trouble in getting the money."

"Oh, Fred is all right."

Granny smiled wisely, but said no more.

Charity and Hope were both dreaming of lovely palaces, and dogs and horses, and golden sovereigns, rolling down the streets.

But Faith slept deeply, and hardly dreamt at all. She only seemed when she woke in the morning to have been talking with her old friend once more. And their talk was not about the money at all. It was about the Comforter.

CHAPTER XIV
FAITH'S GIFTS

IT was only a few days after Faith's birthday that the Great War came to an end, and an armistice was signed by Germany. There were great rejoicings in the village. The church bells rang out all day, flags were erected; the school had a holiday, and there was a bonfire and fireworks at night.

The little girls were very excited, and walked about the village all day talking to everybody. Nobody could keep indoors. They were all shaking each other's hands, and talking about the "wicked Kayser!" A great many wives were rejoicing that their husbands would soon be returning to them.

Faith was only allowed out for a few hours in the middle of the day, but it was wonderful how many came up and shook hands with her, and said how glad they were to see her about again.

"I rather wish I had tumbled out of the tree instead of you," said Hope that afternoon, when they were having tea: "it makes you so important to be ill, and I like being important."

"But it makes you feel so tired," said Faith, plaintively. "I don't feel as if I could run at all, not even from a mad bull."

Hope looked at her reflectively.

"I shouldn't like that," she said. Then with a sudden change of subject, she went on—

"Do you know, Faith, what you could do with your money? It's a lovely idea. And Charlie and I thought of it."

"What? I keep thinking of so many things. I have made a long list already."

"Why, you could buy a beautiful gipsy van, and we could go about the country in it. A caravan. Wouldn't it be lovely?"

"Then we should have to buy a horse, too—a big one—and Aunt Alice would say she couldn't keep him or feed him."

"Oh, Topsy would pull it, or you could buy a horse and feed him. You have enough money to do anything!"

Faith gave a little sigh. She began to feel the responsibility of money weigh heavily on her shoulders. And the very fact of her still being weak and frail made the least thing a burden to her.

That night when she went to bed, Granny came up with her. She and Faith had a little prayer together of thanks for the peace which had come to the world.

And then Faith lying back on her pillows said wistfully:

"Granny, I wish Mr. Cardwell had left me five shillings instead of a hundred pounds. I don't really know how to spend it."

"Yes, I wish he had," said Granny, looking at Faith's white cheeks with great pity; "but, my darling, he would not like to think that it would be a burden to you."

"You see," Faith went on, "Charity and Hope expect me to do something very big with it, and so does Charlie, and it is the big things that are so difficult."

"Now look here," said Granny, cheerfully. "Christmas will soon be here. I know you don't want to spend it all on yourself. Take some of it and buy presents for your friends. Not big presents—just buy nice gifts for them, then put the rest of the money in the bank; and by-and-bye you may think of a nice way to spend it. There is no hurry—you can spend it gradually. There is no need for getting rid of it at once."

"Oh, Granny, thank you so much. If I can do that, I shall be very glad. And do you think I could buy Timothy a very warm thick overcoat? He gets so cold when he goes out at night to see any sick sheep."

"I think that would be a lovely idea."

Granny kissed her, and left her quite happy.

The next morning, she told Charity and Hope of Granny's advice; and though they were at first rather disappointed, they were soon most interested in the list of presents that Faith began to write down.

These were some of them.

Timothy: A very thick overcoat. Granny: A big fur cloak. Aunt Alice: A muff and boa. Miss Vale: A very nice writing case. Mrs. Horn: A warm bed quilt. Mrs. Vale: A pair of gold spectacles. Charlie: A bicycle. Mrs. Cox: A big shawl. Mrs. Budd, who kept the village shop: A china tea-set. Sir George: A pocket-book. Lady Melville: A purse.

There were various children and old women in the village whom the little girls knew. Faith said she would like to give Christmas cakes to them all.

And then came the serious question of what Charity and Hope would like.

Charity said they would like to choose themselves.

"If you don't think it will cost too much money," she said, "I would like a glass book-case, because I'm collecting a library, and by the time I grow up, I shall have a splendid lot of books. And it would stand at one end of our schoolroom. There would just be room for it."

"Oh, what fun it will be buying!" said Faith, clapping her hands. "Of course you can have the book-case. And now Hope?"

Hope walked round the room considering.

"Of course I would really like a big dog," she said; "but Aunt Alice wouldn't hear of that. Why, Faith, I know what we want. That is a proper saddle for Topsy. If you could give me that, we could all ride him."

"But that wouldn't be for you then," Faith objected. "I can give myself that. It can be got for us all, besides the Christmas presents."

And then Hope thought she would like a complete set of garden tools. So Faith put that down.

When once her list of Christmas presents was finished she felt happier. And daily she became stronger, until very soon she was able to take part in lessons again, and in the walks that her sisters took every day.

Time sped away. Aunt Alice wrote to the Pirate about the cheque, and promptly received another back in place of it. December came, a bright, cold December, and they had their first fall of snow. It was too cold to play in the orchard, and they were content to run along briskly out of doors.

At last, a fortnight before Christmas, Aunt Alice said they could all come shopping with her. They were to go to the town early in the morning, have their lunch in a shop, and stay till quite late in the afternoon.

It was a day to be remembered. Never had they so much money to spend. For Charity and Hope felt that they shared with Faith the excitement of choosing and buying all the presents. Aunt Alice was very good in helping them. It was only her own present that was kept secret. And she was as pleased as Faith herself when they chose together a lovely grey cloth cloak lined with white fur, for dear Granny.

Charity got her book-case, and Hope her garden tools. The saddle was chosen and paid for, and then Faith was asked what she was going to get for herself. She could not make up her mind for a long time. At last she saw a picture in a shop which greatly took her fancy. It was a little child being led up a steep hill by a shining angel. Her Aunt smiled when she was told she would like to buy it.

"I might have known something of that sort would have attracted you," she said.

Perhaps the most interesting bit of shopping was ordering the cakes in the pastry-cook's. Faith found that she wanted fifteen, and they had to be made on purpose for her.

Aunt Alice laughed at the woman's astonished face when she took the order.

"It's a good thing you have some currants and raisins at last," she said, "for otherwise it would be no good ordering plumcakes from you."

The little girls asked their Aunt to let them go into one shop by themselves, and Aunt Alice turned her head again, and pretended she did not see where they went.

Faith was very anxious over the set of furs they asked to see. At first the attendant who waited upon them looked rather suspiciously at them.

"These are very expensive," she said. "How much do you want to give?"

Charity looked up with red cheeks.

"We have a hundred pounds to spend, we don't care how much it is."

The attendant smiled. She consulted the head of the fur department. But when she saw that Faith had a little bag stuffed with notes, she became very civil. And the children at last chose a big black fox stole and muff, which cost about sixteen pounds. Faith was rather frightened at the amount, but she paid it, and she went out of the shop wondering if Aunt Alice would be angry if she knew how fast her money was melting away.

It was quite late when all the shopping was finished, and the children were very tired when they reached home.

Granny asked how they had enjoyed themselves.

"It has been just like a fairy story," said Charity, "and I suppose rich people can spend money like Faith has to-day whenever they like. Oh, I do hope I shall be rich one day!"

Granny shook her head at her.

"I wish you better than that," she said; "money is a great care."

"It is indeed," said Faith in an old-fashioned way, "and I never knew it would go so fast, Granny; will you add up for me and tell me how much I have left?"

When bed-time came, Aunt Alice was able to tell her. And Faith was horrified to find that she had only about forty pounds left.

She looked so troubled that Granny came to her. "What is it, darling?"

"Oh, Granny, I wanted to give something out of it to God. I thought you would tell me how."

"But I think many of your presents to the poor old people in the village are offerings to God, dear."

"But I thought in church—I thought Mr. Webster would like to have some."

"To give away to the poor, do you mean? Well, you can talk it over with him, but don't spend it all this Christmas. I advise you to keep some in the bank and take it out when you really need it."

"Yes," assented Faith, "and I won't think about spending it any more, but just enjoy myself."

When Christmas Eve came, the little girls were up early. They took the presents round to the villagers in the morning, and had great fun packing all the cakes into Granny's carriage.

Charlie's bicycle was going to be wheeled along to him after dark. Aunt Alice said she would see to that. Charity's book-case had arrived the day before, but it was not going to be unpacked till after tea, when Faith said she would like to give her presents to the family. The cakes were received with great delight. Mrs. Budd and Mrs. Horn were quite overcome with their presents. Hope said that she and Charity felt the money was theirs, as they helped to give away the gifts, and had the pleasure of seeing the joy they gave.

In the afternoon, Charity and Hope were to leave Faith's presents at the Hall, and she herself staggered up to Timothy's cottage with her big brown paper parcel.

She would allow nobody to carry the coat but herself. It was a bright, frosty afternoon; the woods looked black and silent. In the distance, Faith heard the church bells pealing out. Aunt Alice had gone to help in the decorations at the church. When Faith reached the cottage she found Timothy had just come in. He was hanging up his old coat on a nail behind the door, and turned round with a pleased smile when he saw who it was.

"Come right in, Missie. Eh! 'Tis good to see ye lookin' up agin! Sit ye down now. There be Sandy waitin' to shake hands wi' ye!"

Faith breathlessly held out her big parcel.

"For you, Timothy, with my love and a happy Christmas. I bought it for you myself with some of the money I told you about. Do try it on and see how it fits!"

Timothy slowly undid the parcel. When he unfolded the thick coat, he looked at her with his slow, sweet smile:

"Well, I never did! This beats me altogether. 'Tis fit for the king hisself. However am I to thank you big enough, Missie?"

"Put it on! Put it on!" cried Faith, dancing up and down in her excitement. "I'll help you, Timothy."

So between them, they got Timothy into the coat, and he pronounced it a "perfect fit."

"My last new coat was twelve years agone!" he said.

"Why, that was before I was born," said Faith in awed tones.

"Well, I'm wonderful grateful, Missie! To think that you should give me such a big gift as this! My old bones will ache no more with cold this winter! Dearie me, I shall not know myself!"

He turned himself round and round and Faith admired him amazingly. Then after she had told him the whole history of the purchase they settled down to talk of other things.

"Isn't Christmas a lovely time, Timothy?"

"Ay, Missie, surely it be; and never will there be such a Christmas as this with 'Peace on earth' again. 'Tis like a horrible dream, these four years of killin' and burnin' and drownin'! I always have been fond of Christmas. To us shepherds, when we go round at night, the Message seems to sound out in a partic'lar way, just as it did to them Eastern shepherds. I pray God He will send the Message afresh to the aching hearts in the world to-day to tell them of the joy to be found in the Saviour."

"But it's the Comforter Who speaks to aching hearts," said Faith.

"So 'tis, Missie, and He'll be tellin' them of the One Who loved 'em, and gave Himself for 'em! There'll be those this Christmas who'll be wantin' all the love and comfort they can get. For there be no such sad a time for those who have lost their dear ones, as a real merry-making time all round 'em. It just stabs 'em cruel all the time!"

Faith sat very still on her little stool. She hardly understood Timothy's words, for she was feeling supremely happy herself. Sandy had his nose in her lap, and she was stroking his head.

"I hope there'll be nobody unhappy in our village this Christmas, Timothy. Do you think there will be?"

"We'll hope not, though there is a few with mourning hearts who stiffen their backs, an' will not listen to the Comforter."

"And I suppose if everybody listened, there wouldn't be an unhappy person in the world?" said Faith.

"That there would not," said Timothy earnestly.

When Faith came away from him it was getting dark. He walked over the fields with her and saw her safely into the lane; and she then ran home as fast as she could.

The little cottage was quite gay that night. It was trimmed up with holly and evergreen; there was a beautiful cake for tea made by Aunt Alice. And after tea was cleared away, the presents were produced. Granny was speechless when she saw her cloak, and Aunt Alice was almost distressed when she was given her furs.

"My dear Faith, you ought not to have spent so much money on me!"

But she put them on, and said she felt a duchess in them. The little girls all had Christmas presents from Granny and Aunt Alice. Warm gloves, books, and boxes of chocolates.

When at last the children retired to bed, they were almost worn out with excitement, but very happy. As Granny said when Aunt Alice remarked on Faith's white cheeks:

"Well, Christmas only comes once a year, and this is a year that will be remembered all our lives. We have been pretending for the last four years to feel happy at Christmastime, now we really are."

CHAPTER XV
THE PIRATE'S CHRISTMAS STORY

CHRISTMAS Day dawned bright and clear. After breakfast they shut up the Cottage and all went to church. Dinner was to be late that day, for Aunt Alice was determined not to miss church in the morning.

"We'll have a snack of cold lunch," she said; "and then we'll have a proper Christmas dinner at six o'clock."

The church was very full. Sir George and Lady Melville had their boys home and a party of visitors as well. Charlie was there with his father and mother, but just before the service began, there was a great surprise for the little girls. The Pirate appeared and walked up the aisle, taking a seat on the opposite side to where they sat. Faith nudged her Aunt, and Aunt Alice smiled with a little flush on her cheeks. When they came out of church, greetings took place in the churchyard. Sir George and Lady Melville both thanked Faith very much for her presents, and then Charlie rushed up in great excitement.

"You are a brick!" he said. "You should have heard me yell when I saw my cycle! How did you think of it?"

"We all thought of it," said Faith; "Charity and Hope helped me with everything. Hope said she knew you wanted one."

"It's simply stunning! And I say, I'm going to have a party with fireworks on New Year's Eve, and you're all to come!"

"How jolly!" cried the little girls. "Of course we will."

Then the Pirate, who had been talking to Granny and Aunt Alice, came up, and they all seized hold of him.

"We thought you were in France!" "When did you come back?" "Are you going to stay?"

He laughed.

"I came back last night, and I'm coming to dinner with you to-day. Won't we have fun!"

The little girls of course were entranced.

Then Faith pulled him aside.

"We're having such a lovely Christmas because of the money in the coin cabinet. Aunt Alice says you know about it. Wasn't it the most wonderful surprise for me?"

"I guess it was. Yes, I know all about it. Has it all gone yet?"

"The most awful lot of it has. Wasn't it good of Mr. Cardwell? I do hope he knows how we're enjoying ourselves."

"I expect he does. What have you done to your Aunt Alice? She's looking ripping!"

Faith slipped over to her Aunt's side.

Aunt Alice was wearing her furs, and she was indeed looking her very best. A bright colour was in her cheeks, and a light in her eyes. She took hold of Faith's hand.

"Come along, chicks! We must get home. You will see your Pirate again, so we won't say good-bye."

But Faith had to speak to another of her friends first, and that was old Timothy, who was in the new overcoat and standing outside the gate.

He gripped hold of her small hand.

"A happy Christmas, missie!—But your face tells me you're having that."

"Yes, everything is delicious," said Faith. "Wouldn't you like a week of Christmas Days, Timothy, all bunched together? It goes too quickly for us."

"We can have a week of Christmas joy," the old man said, and then he went off and Faith joined her sisters.

The Pirate arrived about four that afternoon; and he produced out of his pockets the most wonderful presents for everyone. They came from Paris; there were three big chocolate boxes for the little girls tied up with pink satin ribbon; there was a most dainty silk work-bag for Granny, and a tiny little leather box for Aunt Alice. There were dainty handkerchiefs, and scent bottles, and sachets, which were also distributed round.

The children were quite overcome by it all.

"I shall have to write to Mrs. Cox to-morrow," said Charity; "I feel I must tell about it all to somebody."

The Pirate was sitting round the fire with Granny and Aunt Alice.

Aunt Alice every now and then ran away to see how the cooking was getting on, for she had one of the village women to help her for the day, and she wanted some superintendence.

"What is inside your little box, Aunt Alice?" asked Hope presently.

Aunt Alice looked at the Pirate and laughed.

"I will show you after dinner," she said, "not now."

They had a light tea round the fire, and, later on, the children all went upstairs and put on their best party dresses in honour for the occasion.

Dinner, of course, was a great success.

Sir George had sent Granny a huge turkey, there were mince-pies and plum pudding, and apples and nuts and oranges, and a big box of crackers, which was a present from Lady Melville.

And they were all very merry, for the Pirate told them funny stories; some were true, some did not sound as if they were, but they made everybody laugh. And as the Pirate said, this Christmas must be the very jolliest of all, for Peace was amongst them once more.

And then when dinner was over, they all gathered in a circle round the blazing fire, and the little girls besought the Pirate once more for a story. At first he refused, and then he suddenly sat up, and said he would tell them one.

"It was Christmas Eve," he began, "and very dark and cold. A carriage was lumbering up a long drive towards a big gloomy house. Inside was a young man. We will call him Rufus. He did not look happy. He was tired with a very long journey. A few days before he had been busy and happy, for he was doing some hard work, and was told he was doing it very satisfactorily; but suddenly he was told the work was finished, and that he was needed no more. He was glad to come back to his home, and yet he was sorry, for there was nobody to greet him. The only one who had really belonged to him had passed away.

"And when the carriage stopped at the door, Rufus gave a big sigh and walked into the dim, gloomy hall, nodded to the servants, and then went into the library, where he always used to sit and smoke. There was a big fire to welcome him, and a small white terrier. He sat down by it and took the terrier into his arms, and then he kept very still until he began to see pictures in the fire. He saw himself coming into the big house, but flying to meet him was a lady with a beautiful face, and two or three dancing sprites behind her. In the background was another face of an older lady, almost heavenly in its welcoming radiance, and he felt his heart get warm, as warm as his body was getting from the blazing fire. He sprang to his feet and walked up and down the room.

"'I will! I will!' he cried. 'I won't put it off any longer!'"

"What was he going to do?" enquired Charity breathlessly.

"You'll hear. Soon afterwards he went into another room, where he had to eat his Christmas Eve dinner all by himself. But he did not feel lonely any more. He pictured the faces he had seen in the fire round his table. Then he went upstairs after he had dined, and wandered into a great many empty rooms, and planned how he could make them more comfortable. And he went into one particular room, and unlocked a safe in the wall, and took out of it an old-fashioned silver casket; there were precious stones and jewels inside it. He took out one particular jewel, and wrapped it up, and put it in his pocket next his heart, to keep it warm. And then he went downstairs into the hall again, and buttoned himself into his great coat, and jammed on his old felt hat, and away he went down the drive with great swinging strides. His chest was thrown out, and his head well up in the air, for he was determined to be brave. He was going out to meet someone, and he did not know whether he would return to his house that night a conqueror, or a vanquished and despairing man."

"Oh! Was he going to fight an enemy?" asked Hope.

She was hushed up at once by her sisters.

"It's getting most awfully exciting," murmured Charity.

The Pirate went on without noticing these interruptions.

"And then suddenly, when he had got out on the dry, high road, his spirits sank all at once. He remembered how full of hope he had been once before, just before he left for a foreign land; and how he had determined to come off conqueror, but how absolutely he was humbled to the dust; how the desire of his heart was not granted to him. Of course he had said he would win sooner or later, because it was only that horrid big word, 'circumstances' against him. And then he heard a little robin chirping in the hedge, and he bucked up again and went on.

"At last he came to his destination.

"A little, quiet, dark house, with just one light shining out, but that light gave him a cheerful wink, and he got in at the gate and up to the door, and suddenly before he could knock, it was flung open and the one he sought came out."

The Pirate stopped. Aunt Alice bent forward and stirred the fire, and coughed rather loudly.

The Pirate went on a little nervously.

"Well, that's nearly all, children—but he had his interview, and it was well worth all the doubts and fears and tremblings that had beset him before. He went back to his gloomy house in an hour's time, but it was gloomy no more. He came back to it as victor, and it seemed to him as if the whole place was full of glory."

"Is that all?" asked Faith, softly. "And what about the box with the jewel?"

"He kept it for a Christmas present."

"But who was he so frightened of? Who did he go to meet?"

"Ask your Aunt Alice. She will tell you."

But Aunt Alice was looking into the fire. Her hand was shielding her face.

Granny sat back in her chair, and looked smilingly amused. There seemed to be a mystery somewhere.

Suddenly Charity sprang to her feet.

"I know," she said; "Rufus went to meet the beautiful lady. He wanted her to come and live with him as his wife, and he wasn't certain whether she would or not."

"Oh, Charity, you're too sharp altogether!" The Pirate leant back in his chair and laughed.

"Did she say yes?" Hope asked.

"She did," the Pirate said; "she saw how unhappy poor Rufus would be without her. And the next day he went back to her and gave her the ring."

"Was the jewel a ring? Oh, how exciting! And did they marry and live happy ever after?"

"That takes time in the doing," said the Pirate, with twinkling eyes, "but of course that will come to pass."

"And what was the ring like?" asked Hope.

"Ask your Aunt Alice!"

Aunt Alice turned and held up her left hand in the firelight. There upon her third finger sparkled a diamond ring!

And then the little girls gave screams of astonishment and joy.

"Why, you've been telling us about yourself! It's a true story!"

"And you came home yesterday to the Towers."

"And did you come and see Aunt Alice last night?"

"And are you going to take her away from us? We really can't spare her."

"I am going to carry her off to my house, of course. But a pirate sticks at nothing. I shall do more than that. I shall carry dear old Granny off— very gently so as not to hurt her; and then I shall come back for all of you—I shall carry you all off to my gloomy castle, and there you will have to stay. What do you think of that?"

He leant back in his chair and looked at them with a cheerful smile.

It was some time before they could grasp this wonderful news, and when they did, they hardly knew what to say.

"Do you mean," Charity said, earnestly, "that you're going to marry Aunt Alice and take us all to live at the Towers? Why, it will be like a fairy tale. It can't be true!"

"Do you think there will be room enough for you?" asked the Pirate, anxiously.

And then the little girls began to laugh, as they thought of the big, rambling passages, and the large, lofty rooms that were mostly empty.

Bedtime came too soon. But they went upstairs obediently when they were told.

Surely this was the most wonderful Christmas Day that they had ever seen!

The next morning Granny talked quietly about the change in front of them.

The Pirate was coming home to farm his own land. At first, Aunt Alice said she could not leave Granny and her nieces. That sent him away to France very sorrowful, for Granny did not see her way to come to the Towers too. She wanted to stay on in the Cottage with the little girls.

But when he wrote miserable letters saying what a gloomy, empty home he had, and how he longed to fill it with them all, Granny began to think she must give up her own will for his sake, and for Aunt Alice's, and when he arrived at the Cottage in the dark the night before, and Aunt Alice met him at the door, Granny came forward and said she was ready to do anything they wished.

The children listened to this account with the greatest interest.

"What I can't make out," said Charity, "is why you like living here in a tiny cottage better than a lovely house like the Towers, Granny."

"Ah, well," said Granny, smiling a little sadly, "you may understand one day when you are older."

And then she said no more.

A few days after Christmas, the Pirate had Aunt Alice and the children over to tea at the Towers.

They went all over it, and had the joy of settling the different rooms that would be arranged for them. Granny was to have one of the big sunny rooms looking over the green lawns and cedar trees, the little girls were to have a big room next to her for their schoolroom, and then three small bedrooms which led into each other at the end of the passage, were for them to sleep in.

It was bliss to think that they would each have a bedroom of their own.

Aunt Alice was talking to the old housekeeper about some of the downstairs rooms, when Faith stole softly along to the one in which she had first seen old Mr. Cardwell.

The Pirate found her standing by the couch with tears in her eyes.

Turning to him she said:

"Oh, I do wish he was here to see us all. I do miss him so much."

"Why were you so fond of him, I wonder," said the young man, looking at her with tender eyes.

"Oh, he was so unhappy," said Faith, "and then, you know, he got happy, and I liked him better than ever. And he was so kind to me. And he called me 'little Miss Moth.' I shall never, never hear that name again! I did love it so."

"Did you?" said the Pirate, sitting down on a chair and taking her up on his lap. "But you shall hear that name again, for I mean to call you by it."

"Will you, really? Oh, it will be lovely if you do?"

Faith's face was radiant.

"Then come, little Miss Moth, we will go back to the others."

And he and she went out into the big hall, where the Pirate saw once more the picture that had appeared in the fire—his beautiful lady turning with a smiling face to meet him, and two dancing sprites behind her.

www.ingramcontent.com/pod-product-compliance
Lightning Source LLC
Chambersburg PA
CBHW021551150726
47990CB00006B/2493